The Peppermint Pig

By Nina Bawden

The Peppermint Pig
Carrie's War
Squib
The Runaway Summer
A Handful of Thieves
The Witch's Daughter
Three on the Run
The House of Secrets

The Peppermint Pig

by Nina Bawden

Frontispiece by Charles Lilly

J. B. Lippincott Company
Philadelphia and New York

U.S. Library of Congress Cataloging in Publication Data

Bawden, Nina, birth date
  The peppermint pig.

  SUMMARY: Polly, the youngest, finds it difficult to adjust to a sudden
change in the family until she acquires a special pig.
  [1. Pigs—Fiction. 2. Family life—England—Fiction] I. Lilly, Charles, ill. II.
Title.
PZ7.B33Pe3   [Fic]   74-26922
ISBN-0-397-31618-6

Weekly Reader Children's Book Club Edition

In happy memory of my grandmother.

1

Old Granny Greengrass had her finger chopped off in the butcher's when she was buying half a leg of lamb. She had pointed to the place where she wanted her joint to be cut, but then she decided she needed a bigger piece and pointed again. Unfortunately, Mr. Grummett, the butcher, was already bringing his sharp chopper down. He chopped straight through her finger and it flew like a snapped twig into a pile of sawdust in the corner of the shop. It was hard to tell who was more surprised, Granny Greengrass or the butcher. But she didn't blame him. She said, "I could never make up my mind and stick to it, Mr. Grummett. That's always been my trouble."

Of course, I can't be certain Granny Greengrass said this because she died so long ago, years and years before I was born, before there were motor cars on the streets or electricity in the houses or airplanes in the sky, but my grandmother, Emily Greengrass, told me she said it and I believe her, as her children, Poll and Theo and Lily and George, always believed her.

My grandmother was very good at telling stories. Most of her best ones were about the town in Norfolk where she was born and lived until she grew up and married James Greengrass and moved to London. There was one famous tale about a poor swineherd whose pigs had died and whose wife and children were starving. He was in despair until one night a monk appeared to him in a dream and told him that if he dug under a certain oak tree he would find a chest of gold buried there. Poll and Theo had enjoyed this story when they were younger, but now they preferred to hear about Granny Greengrass whose finger had been chopped off by Grummett the butcher. It was more interesting than a fairy story, partly because it had happened in their own family and partly because they were, naturally, a bloodthirsty pair.

Not that they looked it. Poll was nine years old with a soft, rosy face and long, yellow hair the color of duckling's down, and although Theo was ten and a half, most people thought he was younger than Poll because he was so small and thin. "About as thick through as a darning needle," was how their mother, who was a dressmaker, always described him, and his delicate features and wide, shy blue eyes made him look, to anyone who didn't know him, as innocent as a baby angel.

But it was Theo who said, when their mother told them the story about Granny Greengrass for about the hundredth time one dark November afternoon, "What happened afterward? Did she spout *blood?*"

"No, it was a clean cut," their mother said. "Hardly a drop spilled—or no more than when you bite off a young puppy's tail. Or so your Aunt Sarah said. She was there, you know, but not much help by the sound of it. What she should have done was sew it back on, but Sarah never was very practical." She gave a faint sniff. "Though clever at her schoolbooks, of course."

"You'd have sewn it on, wouldn't you, Mother?" Theo said confidently. "What a shame you weren't there! But d'you think the *bone* would have joined up?"

Their mother held up the cambric petticoat she was making for Poll and examined the tucks on the bodice. "That I can't tell. It might have done. She was a big, healthy woman."

Poll said, "What do you mean about biting off puppies' tails?"

"That's what the groom at the Manor House used to do. My mother was cook there, you know. I've seen that groom pick up a new litter one after the other, bite off the tail at the joint and spit it out, quick as a flash. The kindest way, he always said, no fuss and tar-radiddle, and barely a squeak from the pups."

Poll squeaked herself at this thought and Lily, who was rising fourteen, closed her eyes and moaned softly. George, a year older, cleared his throat, pushed his glasses up on his nose, and slammed his book shut. He thought he was too old for his mother's stories now and had been pretending not to listen.

Poll and Theo looked at Lily. She had stopped laying the table for tea and was standing still with closed eyes and a hand on her heart as if she had suddenly been seized by a terrible pain. Lily was a good actress—as good an actress as her mother was a storyteller. When she was certain she had everyone's attention, she opened her eyes, shook her head sadly, and sighed. Then she looked at her mother and said in a soft, reproachful voice, "I really felt quite faint for a minute. Why do you tell them such dreadful tales?"

"She enjoys them herself, that's why," George said. "They've got the taste from her."

"She shouldn't encourage it, then." Lily sighed again, very deeply. "If you must tell them stories, Mother, why don't you tell them something nice? Something that might do them *good?* Read to them out of *Books for the Bairns,* as Father does. Or *On Angel's Wings.*"

"I can't see that a bit of real life does them much harm," Mother said, speaking more mildly than she usually did when one of them criticized her. She was always gentle with Lily and this annoyed Poll, who could never see why she should be. Did she love Lily best? If she didn't, why was she smiling at her like that, as if coaxing her tall, pretty daughter to smile back at her? Oh, it made Poll's blood boil!

George said, "Of course it doesn't." He put his

book down with a bang on the table, making the cups jump, and stood up, stretching and yawning and grinning down at his mother. "No harm at all—as long as they're sitting nice and safe by the fire with the gas lit and the curtains drawn and the tea on the table, Mother's stories just make it seem cozier!"

George was often right about things—which was something else that annoyed Poll occasionally—and he was right about this. Poll and Theo enjoyed dreadful tales because their own lives were so comfortable—nothing dreadful had ever happened to them, nor ever seemed likely to. How could it? Their family's solid brick villa in a leafy suburb of London was the sort people think of when they say *safe as houses* and there was plenty of money to keep them warm and well fed inside it. Their father was a coach painter in the firm of Rowland and Son and his special job was to paint coats of arms on the doors of rich people's carriages. This was delicate work and he was paid three pounds ten shillings a week, which was a good wage at that time, enough for their mother to employ a young maid, called Ruby, to help with the housework and for the girls to have real lace on their drawers, and Theo, a green velvet suit for best with lace on the collar.

They had more important things, too: a lively young mother and a tall, handsome father who spent more time with them than most fathers did. He took them out every Sunday, to Kew or to Hampton Court, and sometimes, on Saturdays, to a fair or a carnival, or to the theater to see Dan Leno the Clown or the Siamese Twins, joined back to back like two stiff little dolls, each playing a xylophone. And he was always bringing them presents, not just on birthdays and St. Valentine's Eve and at Christmas, but on other days, too—and not ordinary presents, either. He used gold leaf for the coats of arms on the carriages and sometimes he brought home small leftover slivers for his children to make Christmas cards with. The week before the dreadful thing happened, the thing that was to change their whole lives forever, he had brought home a tin full, tiny scrapings of real yellow gold, thin as tissue . . .

Poll was the naughtiest one of the family and the dreadful thing happened on one of her naughty days, a dark day of thick, mustardy fog that had specks of grit in it she could taste on her tongue. Theo was not allowed out because of his delicate chest, and by the time Poll got home from school she was already angry. She had been in a cold classroom all day, some of the time stuck in the corner wearing the Dunce's Cap, made of green drawing paper and smelling of gum, while Mother and Theo had been cozy at home, sharing secrets. Poll loved Theo but she was jealous by nature, and when she came coughing in from the fog, hands and feet cold as toads, and found him sitting on Mother's lap by the fire where she wanted to be, she wished he was dead. *She* was supposed to be the baby, wasn't she?

14

She was naughty at tea. Children were expected to behave well in those days and, although Emily Greengrass was less strict in some ways than most mothers, she was firm about table manners. It was always, "Sit up straight," "Don't talk with your mouth full," "Elbows off the table. I won't tell you again."

That afternoon, Poll had to be told once too often. Her mother said, "I've had enough, my girl. Under the table!"

Poll didn't mind. She had eaten as much as she wanted—she always ate a great deal, very fast, unlike Theo, who chewed every mouthful so slowly that Mother's fresh scones, crisp and warm from the oven and dripping with butter, might have been dry lumps of old cardboard—and with a good tea inside her it was pleasant under the table. The starched white cloth hung down almost to the floor, making a good private place where she could behave as she liked and no one could see. The linoleum was brown and patterned in crisscross stripes of a lighter shade. Poll thought these looked like little gates and, pretending to be a baby again, tried to push them open with her fingers. She spat on the floor and blew on the spit, to see the colors change in the bubble. There were spiders in the dusty underside of the table and she fetched one down and teased him by letting him run and then barring his way, until at last she felt sorry and took off her shoe to give him a ride in it.

By this time she was yawning. Someone—George,

probably, he was always kind to Poll when she was punished—had pushed a small green hassock under the table and she rested her head on it. She didn't go to sleep properly, just dozed off and on, listening to the voices above her head and watching the feet round the table through the furry fringe of her lashes: George's heavy shoes, Lily's neat, black buttoned boots, and her mother's slippers that had silver buckles in the shape of small roses.

She must have slept in the end because suddenly her father's boots were where George's had been and his voice was saying, "I am so sorry about this, Emily dear."

Poll was awake at once. Father usually said "Mother." But perhaps it wasn't that startled her but the tone of his voice, which was hoarse and slow as if some of the gritty fog had got into his throat and stayed there.

He said, "Whoever took the money, I was in charge and must be responsible. I should have locked the safe up before I left the office to speak to my father."

"Oh, I knew he'd bring us all down one day," Mother said, and Poll wondered who she was talking about. Dad had said, *my father.* But Grandpa Greengrass was dead . . .

She listened, puzzled and yawning.

Father said, "It's not his fault, Emily. Poor old fellow. If you could see him . . ."

There was a question in his voice. Mother said, "No, thank you, we can't afford two soft hearts in this

16

family! Did Young Rowland know he'd been hanging about?"

"I'm afraid so."

"And accused him, I suppose? Is that it, James? You were afraid he'd send for the police?"

Father said, very slowly and reluctantly, "Yes. Yes, I'll admit I was afraid of that. Even though I was fairly sure Young Rowland was just covering up for himself. He was the only one who was ever alone in the office with the safe open. But it was his word against mine, wasn't it?"

"Old Rowland would take *your* word, James," Mother said. "And you know it."

"Perhaps. In a way, that's the point. The lad's future was in my hands. He stood there, denying what we both knew he'd done, blaming the old man and threatening to send for the police—but with such a look in his eyes! Begging me not to give him away to his father. And I couldn't, Emily! A boy, barely nineteen, with his whole life before him!"

"And yours is behind you, I suppose?"

Poll had never heard her mother speak like that to her father before. Until this moment she had been no more than sleepily interested in what they were saying, as if this were a play going on over her head or a story her father was reading to Lily and George that she didn't quite understand but enjoyed listening to, but now the ice in her mother's voice froze her still under the table.

"Well . . ." Father's boots creaked as he shifted

17

his feet. One of them almost trod on Poll's hand but she was frightened to move. He said, "Well," again. Then, "I can start afresh, Emily. Young Rowland can't. It's his family's firm and he'll have to take over one day. He can't just walk out and get another job somewhere else as I can. And there's his father to consider. Old Rowland. It would break his heart if he knew. His only child."

"You have four children, James." Mother's voice was still cold as winter. "Shouldn't you consider them, too?"

Father cleared his throat. Not, it seemed, to get the fog out of it but in the way George did when he was hurt and embarrassed. He didn't reply and for a moment there was no sound in the room apart from the hiss of the gaslight over the table and the slow, fat tick of the old grandfather clock in the corner. At last Mother said, "I'm sorry I said that. Of course I know that you think of them always."

Father said, "It would be terrible for them to have a father they couldn't look up to. One who had done something he believed to be wrong."

"Yes," Mother said. "Yes, I suppose it might be." She sounded as if she did not altogether believe this but saw no point in arguing further and added, as if changing the subject entirely, "What will you do, James?"

"Something different, I think. Not coach building—that's had its day. In twenty years, Emily, there will be hardly any horse-drawn traffic left on the roads. Everyone will have motor cars."

"I'll believe *that* when I see it," Mother said, and gave one of her sniffs.

Father laughed. "I think you will, and in our lifetime, my dear! What I thought I might do—" his voice lifted suddenly and he sounded young as a boy, young as George—"I thought I might go to America."

Mother said, "James!" and Poll cried out under the table.

"Dad," she said, *"Dad . . ."* fighting her way through the stiff folds of the starched cloth that covered her head, blinding her. Her father lifted the cloth, scooped her up, and held her against him. Safe in the shelter of his arm, she said quickly and angrily before her mother could be angry with her for hearing something she shouldn't have heard, "It's all your fault, Mother. You forgot me. You never said I could come out and I went to sleep under there."

Mother's face was white under her short, red brown curls, and her pretty mouth was buttoned up tight like her tight, buttoned bodice. She was sitting poker straight and staring at Poll.

Poll looked at her, then at her father, who was stroking his dark, silky moustache and watching her gravely. She said, "Why is Dad going away?"

Neither of them spoke. Poll thought they looked scared—scared of *her!* That shocked her, then made her angry. "What's happened?" she shouted, stamping her foot. "Tell me this minute!"

Perhaps most grown-ups would not have answered her—children were supposed to be seen and not heard and were rarely told what their parents were up to—but Emily Greengrass was different. She was a quick, direct person, used to speaking her mind and not mincing her words to make them digestible. She said, "Your father has left his job because there has been trouble in the firm. Money stolen. Not by him, that goes without saying, but for his own, no doubt very good reasons he has taken the blame for it."

Poll guessed that her mother did not think the reasons particularly good ones but knew better than to ask more. She turned to her father. "Are you really going away to America?" Even as she asked this she knew it couldn't be true and started to smile.

But she was wrong: it was true. He shook his head and said gently, "I think so, my little love. Your Uncle Edmund is there, as you know, working on his fruit farm in California. I shall join him to start with. After that . . . Who knows? America is a land of great opportunities. I may make a fortune!" He pressed her hand and gazed beyond her, his eyes bright with dreams in the firelight.

Poll heard her mother sigh, a small, cut-off sound. She tugged at her father's sleeve to bring him back out of his dream and said, feeling hollow inside, "If you go away what will happen to us?"

He looked at her, frowning slightly. "Nothing, my Pretty-Poll. I'll send for you when I'm established, of course. Until then, you will go to my sisters, your Aunt Sarah and your Aunt Harriet, in Norfolk."

Mother stirred and the silk of her dress rustled. She said, drily and politely as if speaking to a stranger, "You've got it all worked out, haven't you, James?" And then, to Poll, "Go upstairs now, it's time. Tell George and Lily to come in here, please, because we must talk to them. And tell Theo to get into bed. I'll explain to him in the morning. I don't want him lying awake all night worrying. You know what an old worry box he can be!" She gave a light, breathless laugh, although there was nothing to laugh at, far as Poll could see, and went on, "Not that there is anything to worry about. Your father knows what is best for us all, you must not forget that. But be a good girl and do as you're told just for once. Into bed and to sleep and not one word to Theo."

"Yes, Mother," Poll said. But she crossed her fingers behind her back as she spoke and kept them crossed while she kissed her parents good night and ran down the passage to tell George and Lily, doing their homework by the range in the kitchen, that they were wanted at once in the parlor. Then she went straight upstairs to tell Theo.

He had hitched his nightshirt over the big solid knob of the brass bed he and George shared and was swinging dreamily backward and forward. Poll had been forbidden to do this because she was too heavy now and might tear her gown, but Theo was lighter than she was. He went on swinging, though more slowly, while she told him what had happened downstairs. His bare legs dangled like pale, peeled willow wands and his thin feet were blue.

"Get into bed," Poll said. "You'll catch your death. It's like ice in this room."

He unhitched his nightshirt and climbed on the high bed, rubbing his feet back to life. His huge eyes shone in the light of the candle like pools of blue water. He said, "Who stole *what?*"

Poll perched beside him, shivering, plumping the soft feather bolster up round her. "Mother said money. Dad didn't say. Only that it was the old man's only son and it would break his heart if he knew. Old Rowland's heart."

She stopped. Old Rowland owned the firm Father worked for. Poll had seen him once. He was a short, stout man with a barrel-shaped belly and a red, jolly face. He had said, "So this is your little maid, James. Pretty-Poll," pinched her cheek, rather hard, and given her sixpence. Poll thought of his heart breaking and saw it, in her mind's eye, like the cracked white pudding basin that had fallen in two halves when Mother dropped it on the stone floor of the scullery . . .

Theo said, "Is that all?"

"Dad took the blame. Owned up . . ."

"To something he hadn't done? That someone else had?"

"I think so."

She wasn't certain. She could barely remember. Dad going away had seemed so much more important.

"Hmmm," Theo said in a funny voice.

"What do you mean, *hmmm?*"

He shook the hair out of his eyes and blinked at her. Then whispered, "Suppose it wasn't ordinary money that was stolen, but gold?" Poll stared, bewildered, and he went on, "Gold *leaf,* anyway. Those shavings he brought home last week for the Christmas cards. In the tin. They're valuable, aren't they? Real gold, he said so."

"Just shavings," Poll said. "What was left over after they'd finished painting the carriages. Like . . . like gleanings in a cornfield."

Poll had never lived in the country but her mother had told her that when she was young she had gone gleaning after the harvest was finished, picking up the fat ears of corn that the farmer's horse rake had missed and left in the stubble.

Theo said, "There was an awful lot though. Pounds and pounds' worth, I'd think. A fortune. If all those scraps were put together and melted down."

He bounced up and down, very excited, squeaking the bedsprings.

"Theo! Dad's not a thief!"

He rolled his eyes upward as if he thought she was too stupid for words. "I didn't quite mean that. Just that perhaps he thought he could take it, like gleanings, and then, later on, someone said, *Where's all that gold gone?*" He grinned at Poll shyly as if wondering if this really made sense (or if it didn't, if he could make her believe that it did), then sighed and said, "He might be scared to say *then,* mightn't he?"

"You're just making a story up. Dad's never frightened of anything. Besides, it was money stolen, Mother said." But Poll was less sure than she sounded. Like Mother, Theo enjoyed telling stories and his were not always true. This one sounded plain silly, Poll thought. On the other hand, Theo was older than she was and everyone said he was clever . . .

He was thinking now, huddled up in the feather bed, chin on his thin, pointed knees. He said, after a bit, "There could be two things, couldn't there? Not connected. I mean this money gone that Dad didn't take and the gold that he *did.* Not meaning to steal at the time, but it would look bad if it came out, as things are."

"I think you're horrible," Poll said. "A horrible, mean, skinny beast."

Theo giggled. "Sticks and stones may break my bones but words will never hurt me."

Poll felt as if she would burst with rage. "I'll tell Dad what you said. I will!"

Theo shook his head solemnly. "You mustn't do that. He'd be upset, thinking you thought he'd really done something wrong."

"It wasn't *me* thought that, it was *you.*"

"He won't know that, will he? Not if you *say* it!"

Poll was muddled by this. She was often muddled by Theo, who had a tortuous mind. Listening to him was like being trapped in the maze at Hampton Court, she thought suddenly—all those paths twisting and turning and no clear way out. She remembered how furious she had been with him earlier when she came in cold and unhappy from school and found Mother cuddling him. She longed to give him a good punch to relieve her feelings but he always yelled when she hit him—sometimes he even yelled when he just thought she was going to—and that would bring Mother up in a temper.

He was looking at her with a nervous expression, as if he knew what she was thinking. Or perhaps he was ashamed of the things he had said and was afraid that she might, after all, tell their father.

He said, "Really, Poll, I think we'd best just keep quiet about it. Not a word to anyone, not even to Lily and George. Dad may have forgotten he brought home that gold. And if you remind him he might feel he's got to own up to that, too—you know how he likes to set us a good example! And stealing gold is worse than stealing money." He was watching her. She stared back until his eyes fell. He said in a hushed voice, "He might go to prison!"

"I'd rather he went to prison than to America. We could visit him and take pies," Poll said stoutly. She had a storybook about a little girl whose father had been sent to prison for debt. There was a picture of the girl carrying a basket full of pies into her father's cell, and the poor, thin father leaping up, holding out his arms and calling her his little angel. Thinking of this picture, and then of her father going to America and being lonely and sad without her, made Poll start to cry. Her throat and eyes burned and fat, warm salt tears rolled down her face.

"*Dad* wouldn't rather go to prison, you juggins!" Theo put an arm round Poll and dabbed at her cheeks with his other hand and the edge of the sheet. "Don't cry, you're not Lily! Dad wants to go to America, you fool. He's wanted to for ages and ages, ever since Uncle Edmund went and started writing letters back. It's an *adventure* for him, don't you see?"

"Old people don't have adventures. It's you that's the fool! And he's going without us, that's what's awful!" Poll felt she would never be able to bear this, she would rather die! "I'll die, I'll *die* if he does, I *won't* go to horrible Norfolk," she cried, banging her fists up and down on the bolster until feathers and dust came out of the seams, making her sneeze.

Theo was snorting with laughter. He said, gasping and snorting, "Of course you won't go if you die, unless you go nailed down in your coffin! But what's wrong with Norfolk? It sounds a good place to me, a good deal more interesting than London, according to Mother."

2

And so it turned out to be . . .

A week later, the four children traveled to Norfolk alone. Mother said it would be easier to clear up the house with them out of the way and she and Father would follow as soon as they could. Until then, the aunts would look after them. "Be good now," Mother said. "Your Aunt Sarah has very high standards."

Aunt Sarah met them when they changed trains at Norwich. Almost dark then, it was quite dark when they reached the town, and the first interesting thing they saw when they came out of the station was a brightly lit butcher's shop, decorated for Christmas with holly and a crib in one window and a live monster in the other—Grummett's Christmas Beast, a great bullock with bloodshot eyes and tight, dark curls between fierce, curving horns, stamping about in his pen and blowing out foggy breath.

"Poor creature," Lily said. "Oh, the poor thing! I think it's dreadful to put him on show when he'll be killed before Christmas."

"Silly-Lily," George said. "You eat meat, don't you?"

Poll and Theo were enchanted. Not only by the beast, but by the chance to press their noses against the window and peer at the very same butcher who had chopped off their grandmother's finger.

"*Is* it the same one, Aunt Sarah?" Theo asked. "You were there, weren't you?"

He looked at Aunt Sarah hopefully. Perhaps she would have a better story than even Mother had told them. She might know what had happened to the chopped finger!

Poll had been thinking along the same lines. She said suddenly, "If he sold it to eat, I expect it would taste like a sausage with bone in it."

"More meaty," Theo said. "They put bread in sausages."

"Shut up," George muttered, looking anxiously at Aunt Sarah. She was tall, like Lily, and as solemnly pretty. Her high, handsome forehead, usually smooth as pale silk, was crinkled now with shock or distress.

She said, "I'm surprised you know about that. My poor mother! No, it's not the same butcher, dear. He passed on some years ago. Although it says Grummett and Son over the shop, he had no boy of his own and the business belongs to Saul Grummett now. His nephew."

"Not *Saul* Grummett?" Theo cried. This was getting better and better! "The one who tried to shoot Mother?"

This was one of her very best stories. Mother had had many young men after her before she got married and Saul Grummett was one. He was a bit of a fool, Mother said, always pestering her, though she'd made it clear she'd have nothing to do with him. Then, one market day, he'd come after her in the town square and shouted, "If you won't marry me, I'll shoot myself and by God I'll take you with me." Mother stood still. Saul meant what he said—he might be a fool but he was a dangerous fool—and everyone in the busy square knew it. He faced Mother, the gun trembling in his hands, and you could have heard a pin drop. Mother looked down the gun barrel and said, "Go and put your father's gun back before he misses it, Saul Grummett. And while you're about it, get your mother to put you safely to bed. I wouldn't have you if you were stuffed with gold."

Theo said, "Dad says, if he'd been Saul Grummett, he'd have let her have it with both barrels." He stopped and added, uncertainly, "That was a joke, of course."

Aunt Sarah had closed her eyes as if she had a bad headache. Opening them, she said, "Grummett is a common name in Norfolk and that was a different Saul

Grummett. He is dead, too, the poor, innocent soul, and glad to be in his grave I would think if he knew you were spreading this shameful story around. Though it's not to *his* shame, altogether. I must say, I'm surprised at your mother."

She breathed deeply to steady herself, then smiled in a determined way, as if it was her duty to smile and she would do her duty whatever it cost her. She said, "Look at the pretty crib, children. Grummett always makes a beautiful Christmas crib."

Theo and Poll inspected the crib without enthusiasm. Mr. Grummett, a whiskery gentleman, saw their innocent faces looking in at his window and smiled cheerily. George was frowning. When they moved on, up the street, he held Poll and Theo back and whispered, "Keep your big mouths quiet, will you? Aunt Sarah is nice, but she doesn't like blood-and-guts talk and it's not fair to tease her."

"I don't care," Theo said. "She's niminy-piminy."

"Well, then. It's not fair to Mother! Aunt Sarah will think . . ."

"Think what?"

But George was still hesitating. As they passed under a street lamp, Poll and Theo saw his face, screwed up and bothered. At last he said, "Oh, never mind. But you know Mother hates being what she calls beholden to people. Well, we're beholden to Aunt Sarah now."

Poll said, "Why?" at once, but George didn't answer because Aunt Sarah had turned back and was calling, "Come along, we're nearly there, children."

"There" was a line of neat brick cottages built in a terrace. Aunt Sarah said, "This is our house, and the one next door is where you are going to live. Aunt Harriet has set tea for you there. We thought it would be nice for you to have tea in your own home after your journey."

The door was open. Aunt Sarah led them through a short, dark, narrow passage to a back room, lit by a brass oil lamp with a white shade hanging above a round table. The room was so small and the table so big that they had to edge round it to kiss Aunt Harriet when she appeared at the door of the scullery.

"Come in, my chicks. Welcome home," Aunt Harriet cried. She was as tall as Aunt Sarah, but her face was brick red and bony instead of soft and pale, and she had sharp, merry eyes, crowfooted with smiling. She hugged them all hard, till they gasped. She said, "What bean poles!" to George and to Lily, and to Theo, "Gracious me, still knee-high to a grasshopper! You're the one takes after your dear little mother, I can see that with half an eye." Theo scowled and Poll was angry on his behalf because she knew how sensitive he was about being so small, but when Aunt Harriet put a finger under her chin and said, "Well, Cherry Pie, got a smile for Aunt Harry?" she couldn't help smiling up at the weather-beaten face that beamed down at her.

31

Theo said, "Where's the bathroom?"

"If you want to pay a visit," Aunt Sarah said, "the closet is out in the yard. Take a candle. And there are washstands upstairs. Hang your coats in the passage and go up to wash before tea."

Aunt Harriet took Theo out through the scullery; Aunt Sarah led the others upstairs. There were two doors at the top, one on each side of the stairs. "Theo and George will sleep in the back bedroom," Aunt Sarah said. "Your mother in the front, and Poll in the boxroom. Lily will stay next door with Aunt Harriet and me. Is that all right, Lily? Shall you mind being apart from the others?"

"Oh, no," Lily said. "I'd *like* that, Aunt Sarah!"

Poll was surprised that she sounded so eager but Aunt Sarah looked pleased. She touched Lily's cheek gently. The flame of the candle bent in the draft and grew tall, filling the front room with huge shadows. Aunt Sarah opened a low door, down two steps in the corner, and said, "Here is your room, Poll, my dear."

It was tiny. An iron bed, a chest of drawers under the window, and a tin bath hanging on the back of the door. "Big enough for a little one," Aunt Sarah said, smiling.

She set the candle down on the washstand in what was to be Mother's room and poured water from the ewer into the basin. "Wash your face and hands properly now, not just a lick and a promise, you're covered in smut from the train. Your trunk has arrived but you need not change your clothes till tomorrow. Just come down when you're ready."

She left them alone. Lily and Poll washed in cold water and dried on a rough, sweet-smelling towel. Poll whispered, "It's a *little* house, isn't it? Our house in London was huge. Where will Ruby sleep?"

Lily said, "Sssh . . ." and glanced over her shoulder. She whispered back, "Ruby's not coming."

George was scrubbing his face with the washcloth. He put out his hand for the towel and said, "We can't afford a maid now. Don't be stupid, Poll."

"I'm not stupid. Why can't we afford one?"

George sighed. He and Lily looked at each other over Poll's head and she was suddenly angry because they seemed to know something she didn't know.

George said, "I did try to explain . . ."

"*Mother* should have done," Lily said. "Why everything is always left to me, I don't know! Listen, Poll! Dad hasn't any money now he's not working and he won't have any for ages and ages. All our furniture has to be sold to pay for his ticket to America—that's why he and Mother have stayed behind now—and Aunt Sarah will have to pay for *us,* for the present. The rent for this house, and our food, and . . . oh, everything!" She spoke in a low, scolding voice as if all this was in some way Poll's fault. Poll stared at her, sullen faced, hating her. Lily said frantically, "Don't you understand? If it wasn't for Aunt Sarah, we'd be in the workhouse!"

"Don't frighten her, Lily," George said. "It's not

33

quite true, anyway. Mother will have a bit of money left from the sale. And she can do dressmaking—she says lots of her old customers will be glad to know she's back in the town. But Aunt Sarah will have to help to begin with. She doesn't mind, Dad says she likes to help people, but it's only fair to be grateful. So try to be good, Poll."

"I'm always good," Poll said stiffly.

"Try to be better, then." George grinned at her. "Don't kill yourself over it, just think before you speak. Count ten. That'll do for a start."

"If you don't," Lily said, "you may still end up in the workhouse."

They went downstairs. The back room was cozy after the chill of the bedrooms. Aunt Harriet sat in front of the fire, skirt hitched up because of the heat, making toast with a three-pronged brass fork. There was toast and dripping for tea, potato cakes with golden syrup, and fat, sticky biscuits full of caraway seeds. Aunt Sarah poured tea. It was very weak, the kind of tea Mother called "water bewitched." Poll thought of saying this, then counted ten and decided she had better not mention it.

She looked at her aunts. Aunt Sarah had a sweet, gentle face but it was somehow stern, too. Aunt Harriet's face was much jollier. She had thin hair, fine as spider's thread, twisted up in a skimpy bun on top of her head, and a loud, abrupt laugh, like a man's. Impossible to imagine Aunt Sarah laughing, Poll thought;

it would make her face too untidy! But she smiled at them all with great kindness. She said, "We must discuss your education, children. I expect the first thing you will all want to know is where you are going to school."

It was the last thing Poll wanted to know. School was being rapped over the knuckles with a ruler and being stood in the corner, Dunce's Cap on and fenced in with a blackboard that would fall over if she moved as much as an inch. But when she had counted to ten, she knew she had better not say so. She munched toast and dripping and sighed.

Aunt Sarah said, "George will go to the grammar school, of course. Theo to the boys' school just round the corner, and Poll to my school."

Aunt Sarah was headmistress of the girls' school and Aunt Harriet taught there as well. Her eyes crinkled into bright slits as she said to Poll, "I wish you could be in my class, Cherry Pie, but I only teach babies."

Aunt Sarah said, "It is Lily we must think about. What do you want to be when you grow up, my dear?"

"Mother thinks I should be a nurse. Or go into the post office. But I would like to be an actress, really." Lily blushed. "It is my greatest wish."

Poll was astonished to hear her say this to Aunt Sarah. It always made Mother angry! "If wishes were horses, then beggars would ride," was what Mother said.

But Aunt Sarah was smiling. "That is a fine ambition, Lily. You get it from your dear father, of course. He was always so fond of the theater. There is a private school in Norwich with a good reputation for drama. Perhaps we can manage to send you there. You will have to work hard, of course. George, too. There is nothing you can't do if you work hard enough. You can become a great actress and George can get a scholarship to Cambridge and become a professor . . ."

As she spoke she stopped smiling and her eyes seemed to look beyond them, out through the walls of the little, hot room, and Poll was reminded of her father, dreaming of making his fortune in America. Aunt Sarah was gazing into the future as he had gazed into the fire, seeing them not as they were now but as they would be one day if she had a hand in it, grown up and out in the world, famous people . . .

Aunt Harriet laughed her loud, cheerful laugh. "And what about Theo here? He's not going to come to much if he doesn't eat more. One potato cake, and half of *that* left on his plate! No wonder he looks pale as lard."

"I'm not hungry," Theo said.

"You need a good purge, my boy! A good dose, that'll bring the color back into your cheeks. Senna tea or prune paste, which would you rather have?"

Theo shook his head, looking as if he might be sick any minute.

"Not tonight, Harriet," Aunt Sarah said. "The boy

needs his sleep more than anything else. They all do."

"I'm not tired," Poll said, though she was. So tired, suddenly, that she could barely keep her eyes open, too tired to protest when Lily led her upstairs and helped her undress in that strange little room with the tin bath on the back of the door that looked like a humpy whale in the candlelight. "It's like going to bed in a cupboard," she said when Lily tucked her in and kissed her good night.

Lily laughed and kissed her again and whispered, mouth so close that it tickled Poll's ear, "I'm sorry I teased you about the workhouse, darling Poll. I didn't mean it, not really."

Poll thought about it though when she woke: about being poor and shut up in a bleak building with bars on the windows, and eating workhouse gruel, and wearing a gray workhouse uniform, and walking out two by two in a long crocodile, but she said nothing about it, not even to Theo. It began to seem like a rather shameful dream she had had and, like a dream, it would have faded away in the end if they had not met Mrs. Marigold Bugg . . .

That was only their fourth day in Norfolk but they had done so many things it seemed they had been there for weeks. Aunt Sarah had taken them on a tour of the town, shown them the Assembly Rooms, the wide, paved Market Square, the beautiful church, with a roof that was full of flying wooden angels, and the family graves in the churchyard. Mother's parents were buried there, and old Granny Greengrass. Theo asked, "Where's *Grandpa* Greengrass?" but Aunt Sarah didn't answer. Instead, she hurried them back into the church and showed them the carvings of the Swineherd with a baby pig tucked under each arm, and told them the story they already knew, about how he had found a great treasure under an oak tree and built the church spire as a gesture of gratitude. "His duty to God," Aunt Sarah called it.

Aunt Sarah was all duty; Aunt Harriet all temper and fun. A walk with Aunt Sarah was always a lesson; with Aunt Harriet it was an adventure. She marched them over open, bare heathland and through woods and plowed fields where they had no business to be. She had no patience with private property; notices that said TRESPASSERS WILL BE PROSECUTED were invitations to her and she always carried a penknife in her pocket to help herself to whatever was going, even if it was only a turnip.

She bought hoops for the two younger children: a wooden hoop for Poll and an iron one, with a hook called a skimmer, for Theo. "Wooden hoops are for girls, iron hoops for boys, don't ask me why," Aunt Harriet said. Poll couldn't make up her mind which she liked best. A wooden hoop was free-running, which was more exciting in some ways because it had a wild life of its own as it bounced in and out of the ruts in the road, but an iron one made a lovely hissing sound that turned into a singing hum if you ran fast enough. The day they met Mrs. Bugg they had bowled their hoops for miles, Aunt Harriet breathless behind them, and were crossing the square on their way home, dusty and happy and hungry for tea.

Mrs. Marigold Bugg was tall, the same thickness through from shoulders to knees. As she came toward them she seemed to sway rather than walk, with a boneless, wavy motion that made Poll think of a caterpillar. Aunt Harriet took Poll's hand and quickened her step, and Poll had the feeling she would have marched them straight past without speaking if Mrs. Bugg had not said, "Good afternoon, Miss Harriet. What remarkably mild weather we're having."

Aunt Harriet stopped. They talked for a minute about the warm weather. Then Mrs. Bugg said, "So these are poor Emily's little ones!" She gave Poll and Theo a smile that had no friendliness in it. "Your mother and I are old friends. It broke my heart to hear of her trouble."

Aunt Harriet said, "This is Mrs. Bugg, children. She and your mother were dressmaking apprentices together."

Mrs. Bugg weaved her head backward and forward. Poll thought, *Not a caterpillar, a snake! A snake that is going to strike!* The snake hissed, "Poor little fatherless things!"

Aunt Harriet held Poll's hand so tight that the

39

bones ground together and she had pulled the corners of her mouth down in the way she did when she was angry.

But it was Theo who spoke. "We're not fatherless, Mrs. Bugg. My father is going to America to make his fortune."

Mrs. Bugg's thin, pale lips smiled as if she knew better. She said, in a voice that tried to be sad but had a gleeful sound running through it like a stream bubbling, "Poor, brave little boy! Poor Emily, too, how will she bear it? She was always so proud. And it must be a worry, Miss Harriet, for you and your sister. All this on your plate when you have enough there already! I would never have believed James would do such a thing, but I suppose blood will out!"

She was overacting as Lily did sometimes, Poll thought, but Mrs. Bugg wasn't as pretty! In fact she was *hideous,* with her small, green, pinpoint eyes and her small, swaying, snake's head. And in spite of her kind concern she was glad that Father was going away and meant them to know it! Oh—she was *rude!* Poll looked at Aunt Harriet hopefully, expecting her to be rude back, as she could be when roused, but although her aunt's pulled-down mouth showed her temper, there was no sign of it in her voice. "Sarah and I are only too glad to have James's children living so close for a while. It will be a sad day for us when he sends for them to go to America."

"Do you really think that he will?"

Aunt Harriet laughed as if this was a ridiculous question, not worth an answer, and said, "It's nice to talk, Marigold, but I mustn't keep the children hanging about, they'll get cold. I hope your father is well, and young Noah. I thought he looked poorly last time I saw him, as if he was outgrowing his strength."

She didn't wait after that but swept the children away, walking so fast that they had to run to keep up with her and not slowing down until Theo tugged at her coat sleeve and gasped, "Aunt Harry, what did she mean, *blood will out?*"

Aunt Harriet said, "Oh, she's a silly, sour creature, don't bother your head with her blather."

"She couldn't *ever* have been Mother's friend," Poll said. "She's too mean and she's *old.*"

"Only a couple of years more than your mother. If she looks older it's because she's had a hard time of it. Husband and two babies dead of consumption, only Noah left now. But you're right, she and your mother were never friends, really. Especially not after your mother and father were married. Marigold would have liked to marry James herself, that's the truth of it, but he barely knew she existed. The day of the wedding she went to her bed for a month and refused to get up until her father took a strap to her. After that she quite lost her looks—not that they were all that much to begin with . . ."

Theo said, "You haven't answered my *question.*"

"You've had all the answer you're going to get,"

Aunt Harriet snapped, letting her temper loose suddenly like an angry dog she had been holding back on a lead until now. "Children should be seen and not heard. Don't you know that?"

They said nothing. When Aunt Harriet looked and sounded this way it was best to keep quiet. Or else change the subject. Poll said, in an affected, surprised voice, "Look—there's Lily! Without her coat on!"

Lily was running toward them, pinafore fluttering, copper curls bouncing. "There you are! Where have you been all this time? Mother and Father have come. They've been here simply *ages.*"

Father's boat was sailing on Christmas Eve. Only two days away, but they would have all tomorrow together. He made it seem like a long, lovely holiday. "We'll do a grand tour," he said, "see all there is to see. Hire a trap from the Angel and do things in style."

And as the church clock struck ten, he was there at the door with a smartly painted trap and a shiny black pony. They were all dressed in their best: Mother in her bustled coat trimmed with jet beads at the edges, the boys in Norfolk jackets and knickerbockers, the girls with lace petticoats over their flannel ones, stiff, new buttoned boots and creamy wool coats that had little fur collars. Father handed them into the trap, tucked the rug over their knees, and said, "My three girls look like princesses."

It was a fine day with a pale wintry sun and a new

frosty nip in the air. As the trap rattled along a little breeze blew back the sweet, leathery smell of well-polished harness and the dusty, warm, oily smell of the pony. To Poll's ear, his hooves beat out the tune, *Father is going away tomorrow, Father is going away* . . .

The town square was bustling with people. Father and Mother greeted those that they knew, bowing to right and to left as if they were royalty. "There's Miss Gathergood, James," Mother said. "Gracious me, hasn't she aged? And Pamela Slap—and old Mr. Mullen I used to work for. The buttonholes I've made for that man! Stop the trap, dear, we can't pass without speaking, and he will be interested to know you are off to America. Sit up straight, boys, do me credit now. Poll, don't look so miserable. Have you a stomachache?"

Poll shook her head. She did have a pain but it wasn't that kind. Nor was it something she could speak of to Mother because she was partly the cause of it, sitting there in her best clothes and looking so cheerful and pretty and proud as she told Mr. Mullen that Father was leaving them. Smiling as if she were happy about it!

"So I'll be a grass widow, Mr. Mullen. Not for long, of course, but I daresay time will hang heavy sometimes."

"If it does," Mr. Mullen said, "maybe I can put something your way." He looked at her solemnly and the children looked at him. They had heard about old Mr. Mullen, who kept a general store and employed several girls to make dresses for his customers in a big room above it. "A slave driver," Mother had called him, "a wicked old devil," but he looked a meek, harmless man with a pink, knobbly nose and a mole on his chin that had several black hairs growing out of it. He said, "Business hasn't been the same since you left, Mrs. Greengrass. Sixteen years—and Lady March still says no one can fit a dress as you did."

Mother pursed her lips to stop herself smiling. "Well, I'll have to see, Mr. Mullen. It's early days yet. These four young ones keep me busy, you know, so I can't promise anything."

"Don't overdo it, Mother," Lily said when Mr. Mullen had lifted his hat and walked on, "or he'll think you don't want to work for him."

"He'll pay me better if he thinks I don't need it," Mother said. "I know the old rascal. And that Lady March! Mean as two sticks and not only with money. Never a word of praise to your face."

Father laughed. "Plenty behind your back though, it seems. And you look pleased about it, so don't pretend not to be."

"It's nice to be remembered," Mother said smugly.

And she was, it appeared. Now the trap was stationary, several people came up to them, were introduced to the children, talked of old times. Most of them had not seen Mother and Father since they were married—was that really 1886, *really* so long ago?—or at least since the two children were babies and Mother had brought them to stay with the aunts for a holiday.

Lily and George listened to these conversations more patiently than Theo and Poll, who began to feel that the last precious day with their father was slipping away like sand through their fingers. The young pony was fidgeting, too, tossing his head up and down and clattering his bit. Poll started humming under her breath and twisting her head round. Her father saw this and nodded to her mother to finish what she was saying. Poll said, interrupting, "Look, there's that Mrs. Bugg, Theo."

She was coming toward them with her strange, swaying walk, a tall boy beside her. Mother said, "Wait, James, we can't drive off now, she'll think we are cutting her. I must have a word with the poor soul, if only a minute."

Mrs. Bugg had called Mother poor, Poll remembered. *Poor Emily.* But Mother had sounded kind, Mrs. Bugg hadn't . . .

She put her hand on the side of the trap. She looked at Mother with her pinpoint green eyes. Then at Father. She said, "So you're leaving the country, James."

Father smiled. "On business, Mrs. Bugg. How are you keeping? And Noah?"

Noah was a long, rangy boy with a small head and small ears, like his mother's. His eyes were green, too, but larger and lighter, like ripe dessert gooseberries.

Mrs. Bugg said, "Speak up, Noah."

He said, "Mornin'," and hung his head.

Mother said in an encouraging voice, "Noah must be the same age as Theo. I remember when Sarah came to stay after Theo was born she said you'd just had a boy. They'll be in the same class at school, I expect. Do you like school, Noah?"

He looked up at her through his long lashes and tittered.

Mrs. Bugg said, "He and your Theo don't look the same age though. You'd hardly credit it, really. My great boy and your little, pale fellow. You must have been worried sick many a time, wondering if you were going to rear him."

Noah tittered again, hand in front of his mouth, gooseberry eyes watching Theo, who turned away, pretending not to be listening.

"Theo's small but he's strong; he'll grow when he's ready," Mother said. "Are you still working at Mullen's, Marigold? Is he still an old devil? No sign of it when we spoke a few minutes ago, we were far too grand with each other. *Yes, Mr. Mullen; yes, Mrs. Greengrass.* Lifting his hat, mild as milk, and I suddenly thought how he used to lose his temper with us, rushing into the sewing room shouting and swearing and waving his stick because we girls were making more noise than he liked, and how we used to tease him sometimes and it was all I could do to keep a straight face!"

"I'm afraid I have to nowadays," Mrs. Bugg said. "In my position I can't afford to laugh at old Mullen any more than I can afford to dress up to the nines every day and go swanking about in a carriage."

She weaved her snake's head about and gave a short, hissing laugh as if she were making a joke, but Poll knew she meant to be spiteful.

Mother's smile faded. "I make all our clothes, as you must know, Marigold, and the trap is hired by the hour." She looked hurt and ashamed and it made Poll so angry she thought she would like to kill Mrs. Bugg.

After that, although they all talked and laughed a great deal as the trap rattled through country lanes, the fat pony's feet going *pat, pat, pat* in the dust, it was only to keep one another's spirits up. Mrs. Bugg had made them feel foolish, as if it were showing off to dress up in their best clothes and parade through the town when it wasn't a Sunday, and all four children were glad when the expedition was over and Father set them down at their door. He and the boys took the trap back to the Angel, Lily ran straight into Aunt Sarah's house without speaking, and Poll followed Mother upstairs to her bedroom.

Emily Greengrass peeled off her gloves and said, half to Poll, half to herself, "Well, I deserved that, didn't I? Made a fine fool of myself, peacocking about like a lady when I haven't a penny to bless myself with." She scowled at herself in the mirror as she unpinned her hat and lifted it off and jabbed the long pins into the crown.

Poll came up behind her and looked at her face in the glass. She said, frightened, "Don't cry."

"I'm not," Mother said. "Goodness me!" But her voice shook, and when she turned and grabbed Poll and held her pressed close, Poll could hear her breath creaking unevenly through her boned bodice. She cried a little herself, in sympathy, until Mother said, "There, that's enough. Turn off the waterworks now and don't let your father know we've both been so silly. He's got enough to bear, leaving us all, without you and me making things harder with a lot of old misery. So let's put a good face on it and send him off happy."

3

The little front sitting room of the cottage was furnished with what was left from their London house. Most of the valuable things had been sold, the grandfather clock and the round walnut table and the pretty Chippendale chairs, but the bookcase with the brass inlay and the secret drawer that flew open when you pressed a knob at the side was brought down to Norfolk, and Mother's treadle sewing machine, and the old leather sofa that had been kept in the kitchen in London because it was too shabby for the parlor. "We'll have it under the window," Mother said. "It'll do as a lookout post."

The cottages had long, thin gardens at the back; their front doors opened onto the Market Square. Kneeling on the slippery sofa was rather like having a permanent seat at the theater because something was always happening outside the window: people going to shop, or to church, or to the bakehouse with pies to bake for dinner; farm carts and Gypsy carts passing; foxhounds off to the meet; the Salvation Army band playing at least twice a week; the Town Crier, dressed in his robes and calling "Oyez, oyez," before he cried out his message.

The week after Christmas, a man with a dancing bear appeared in the square. Someone had given the bear beer to drink and he stood on his hind legs, waving his great black head and swaying from side to side like a drunken sailor. Lily said it was cruel, to give a poor bear alcohol, but Poll and Theo thought he seemed happy enough and went outside to take a closer look.

As they slammed their front door, the station cab drew up and a short, fat man got out of it. Poll glanced at him briefly and ran round the back of the cab. Theo caught hold of the back of her pinafore. He whispered, "Poll, who's that man?"

She answered absently, watching the bear who had little, red eyes and long, cruel-looking claws like steel rakes, "I don't know. Yes, I do. It's Old Rowland, I think. Oh, I am glad he's wearing a muzzle!"

Theo said, *"What?"* and she laughed.

"I mean the bear, silly!"

"Poll!" He sounded so shocked that she dragged her eyes away from the bear. Theo's face had gone white. He said, "Go and talk to him, Poll. I'll warn

Mother," and was off like a shot round the end of the terrace of cottages, to go in the back way.

Poll looked after him, puzzled. But she had never been shy and Old Rowland had once given her sixpence. The cab had moved off and she went up to him, thinking that if she smiled at him nicely he might give her sixpence again. If he did, she would give it to the man with the bear when he came round with his cap.

She said, "Hallo, Mr. Rowland," and he looked down at her, his fat neck rolling in red, bristly folds over his collar. Something about him was different but she couldn't think what.

He said, "Why, it's James's little maid, isn't it? Pretty-Poll."

She smiled, wondering if he would remember that the last time he had called her Pretty-Poll he had given her sixpence, but he only shook his head, sighing as if the sight of her had made him feel sad, and said, "Is your mother in?"

The front door opened. Mother stood there, rather flushed, one hand touching her hair. Old Rowland said, "May I come in, Mrs. Greengrass?" He had taken his hat off and was holding it in front of him, looking humble.

Mother nodded and stepped back. She said, "Poll, take Mr. Rowland into the front room while I make tea."

Old Rowland stood aside to let Poll go first

through the door as if she were a lady. This embarrassed her and she stood awkwardly on one leg, rubbing an itchy chilblain on the back of her calf with the toe of her boot. Old Rowland looked round the room, then at Poll. He said, "Shall we look out of the window? It's a long time since I've seen a dancing bear."

He stood beside Poll while she knelt on the sofa and pressed her nose against the cold glass. The bear was on four legs now, shambling beside his owner who was going round with his cap. The audience was dwindling rapidly. Poll said, "I do think it's mean of people to go away without paying, don't you?"

Old Rowland didn't take the hint. Instead he sighed as he had done before and said, "Do you like living here, Pretty-Poll?" and she knew what was different about him: he had been such a jolly man the last time she had seen him and now he looked like a sad one.

She said, because it was polite to try and cheer up visitors when they were miserable, "Oh, yes, we all do, even Lily. She likes being next door with Aunt Sarah because she can get on with her homework without being bothered by Theo and me. And *I* think it's more fun than living in London, especially now it's turned cold. Aunt Harry says, soon as the ice holds she'll take us skating."

He looked at her stupidly. "Don't you miss your father?"

This was such a silly question she wasn't sure how to answer. Anyone would miss their father if he had gone to America, surely Old Rowland knew that? "Well," she said cautiously, "he hasn't been gone very long."

"No," he said. "No, I suppose not."

Mother came in with the tray. She had borrowed Aunt Sarah's best Lowestoft china. She said, "Would you like something to eat, Mr. Rowland? You must be hungry after your journey from London."

She put the tray down on a table that had escaped being sold because one leg was rickety and smiled at him very stiffly and coldly.

Old Rowland gave one of his heavy sighs. "When you know what I've come to say, Mrs. Greengrass, you may not want to offer me anything. Trouble is, I hardly know how to begin . . ."

Mother said, "Please sit down first, then. I think *that* chair will hold you. I'm afraid we're not quite straight yet; we're still waiting for the rest of our furniture." She gave Poll a sharp look, warning her not to deny this, and added, "Perhaps it will save time, Mr. Rowland, if I say at once that I know what you've come to tell me and that I am glad about it, even if it's too late to be of much use, of course."

He shook his head and his drooping jowls quivered. "James knew the truth all along, did he? *I* should have known! Mrs. Greengrass, why didn't he tell me my son was a thief? And worse—that he'd let your good man take the blame?"

He was blowing and puffing as if he had been

running a race. If he had not been so old, Poll might have thought he was going to cry. Mother's stiff look softened and she moved quickly toward him, hands outstretched, as if he were one of her children in trouble. She said, "Oh, you poor man, he wanted to spare you, what else?" Old Rowland took her hands and bowed his head over them. She looked at Poll over his bent head. "You go and find Theo."

Poll went. She closed the door and waited outside for a minute but she couldn't hear anything clearly, only her mother's voice rising and falling in a gentle, comforting murmur and then a strange heaving, gasping sound that was Old Rowland crying. Poll felt the hot blood come up in her face and ran into the kitchen, through the scullery, and out into the garden, so fast that her cheeks shook.

Theo wasn't in their garden. Poll ran to the end, slipping on the iced-up puddles in the dirt path, looked through the hedge, and saw him by Aunt Sarah's summerhouse, crouched on his haunches and scrabbling beneath it. She banged open the wooden gate between the two gardens and shouted, "What are you doing?"

Theo sat back on his heels. His blue eyes were glittering and his fair curls were damp on his forehead. He whispered, "Getting rid of the evidence."

"What do you mean?"

Aunt Sarah's summerhouse, a little room built for her to be private in, with a desk and a bed and a fireplace in one corner, was raised from the ground on brick blocks. Theo pushed earth underneath and banged it flat with his hand. He said, "That gold leaf. Just in case that's what he's come for."

"I don't think it is." Poll drew a deep breath and said, amazed, "He's just standing there *crying!*"

Theo didn't appear to have heard her. He said, "I had to bury it here because the ground's frozen up everywhere else. I didn't know what to do at first. I mean, he might have wanted to search the house, mightn't he, to look for the gold Dad had taken? Then I remembered the Swineherd." Theo stood up, brushing dirt from his knees. "You know, I expect that's what really happened in that old story. It wasn't fairy gold that was found, but real gold that was stolen by someone and hidden. Perhaps the Swineherd stole it himself and then wondered how he could possibly explain to his neighbors why he'd got rich so quickly. So he thought up that mad tale about a monk coming to him in a dream and telling him that if he dug under the oak tree he'd never be poor any longer. The Swineherd spread this around for a bit until everyone got used to the idea, then simply produced the gold that *he'd* buried and pretended his dream had come true!"

Theo pushed his hair back and looked very pleased with himself. "Clever when you think of it, really! Did you say Old Rowland was crying?"

Poll nodded, bewildered.

"Whatever for?"

"I'm not sure."

"Didn't you listen?"

"Only for a bit. Mother said she knew why he'd come. Then *he* said, why hadn't Father told him? About Young Rowland, that is."

She stopped. It was clear in her head that Father had been brave and kind and too fond of Old Rowland to want him to know that his only son was a thief, but when she wanted to put this into words she began to feel muddled: she was sure there was something more to what had happened than that. It was rather as if there was a missing piece of a puzzle locked away in a drawer at the back of her mind and she had somehow mislaid the key to it. "It was nothing to do with your old tin of gold, anyway," she said scornfully.

"I don't see how you can be so sure," Theo said. They had been too busy moving house to make cards this Christmas and he had kept the tin of gold leaf in his toy box. When Old Rowland appeared it was the first thing he thought of and he had rushed upstairs, sick with terror, to find it and hide it. Now he had buried it safely his fear was fading fast like a bad dream in daylight, but he had enjoyed the feeling of acting so quickly and bravely and was reluctant to admit it hadn't been necessary. He said, arguing with himself as much as with Poll, "After all, there was no need for Dad to go away if he didn't feel just a bit guilty about *something.*"

"You said he wanted to go to America," Poll reminded him. "He wanted an adventure, you said."

"I know I said that. And I think that he did. I

know *I* wouldn't want to stay stuck in the same place all my life. But it's not enough of a reason for leaving his job like he did. I mean, it just isn't *enough* . . ." He struggled with the impossibility of making it clear what he meant, gave up, and rounded on Poll. "You ought to have *listened*."

She stuck her nose in the air. "Eavesdropping's wrong."

"Oh, don't be a prig! How else can we find out what's happening? Grown-ups only ever tell you part of a thing, you know that. What they think suitable. And it's no good at all *asking*. Not Mother, because it'll only upset her to think about Father, and if Lily and George know more than we do they'd never tell us, and Aunt Sarah would just pretend she'd not heard what we said, and Aunt Harry . . ."

"Do shut up," Poll said. "Is Dad coming back? That's all I want to know, really."

He looked at her, seeing her mouth turning down at the corners, not miserably, but in the mulish way that had always got her into trouble at school and sometimes made even the kindest of people call her stubborn and willful, and knew that she had suddenly grown bored with all this talk about something she couldn't quite understand and that if he went on about it she would fly into one of her rages.

He said quickly, "Of course he will. If you're thinking about what that horrible woman said, what does she know about it? That horrible Bugg!"

This made her giggle as he had known it would. "She walks like a caterpillar, did you see that? Like this, look . . ."

She went round the side of the summerhouse, wriggling her shoulders and bottom and snaking her head about, looking so strange that Aunt Harriet, coming up the path with an armful of coats and scarves, stopped and stared. "What *are* you doing, child?"

"I'm being a caterpillar," Poll said with her sweetest smile. "A beastly caterpillar bug."

Aunt Harriet beamed at what seemed to her childish nonsense. "Are you, dear? Well, stop it now and get your things on; we've all been looking for you and the others have given up and gone on ahead with Aunt Sarah. Everyone says the ice is thick enough now at Eel's Pit."

It was the first time that winter. The weather, so mild up to Christmas, had become in the last week what grown-ups called "worse" and the children had been waiting hopefully, looking at the windows when they woke in the morning to see if they were still frosted over and testing the ponds every day. Now half the town was out on Eel's Pit, sliding or skating, dogs barking wildly, toddlers squealing as they clung to their mothers or bumped down on their well-padded bottoms. Poll and Theo saw George, staggering round like a lunatic clown on some old skates of Father's, and Lily, on new skates Aunt Sarah had bought her, was pushing an old chair uncertainly over the ice.

"Pity you two haven't got skates," Aunt Harriet said. "Not worth it while you're still growing. Still, you can have fun on the slides."

She put her own skates on. As soon as she stood up, she was surrounded by little girls from her class at school, bundled-up gnomes with knitted hats and red cheeks, shouting, "Miss Harry, Miss Harry, take me . . ." She laughed and went sailing away like a great heavy bird, pulling a sliding child in each hand, the others running and slipping and screaming behind her. The wind blew her long skirts and lifted her dark mannish hat until it stood on its pins in a vertical halo.

"Come on, Theo," Poll cried. She dashed at the ice and it slid squeakily away under her, throwing her flat on her back, legs in the air. Theo pulled her up, laughing. "You've got to start slowly. Try a proper slide, watch the others."

There were two slides for the bigger children who didn't have skates: a short one by the fence, and a longer one that went the full length of the pond, under the trees. Theo made for this one and Poll followed him. He said, "It's only for boys, can't you see? That's the girls' slide over there, by the fence."

Poll saw at once that the boys' slide was not only longer but better, made faster by strong, hobnailed boots. She pulled her mouth down and went on toward it but stopped when she got there. The boys were all bigger than she was, and very much bigger than Theo. They let him join in though; he took his turn and shot down the slide, a fearful joy in his eyes. He tottered a bit at the end but kept on his feet. "Oh, it's *fast*," he said, as he passed Poll to take his place in the line. Poll watched him angrily. Why shouldn't she join in too? There was no law, was there, saying NO GIRLS ON THIS SLIDE? She pushed her way in, before Theo, and took off with a running start, cold air solid in her mouth, ice glassy smooth under her feet, slipping backward. There was a marvelous moment halfway when she knew she was going to make it and from then on it was almost like flying, a lovely, free feeling. She ran back to the start and went down twice more, straight and quick as an arrow. No one tried to stop her and though some boys laughed she was too happy to care. Then, the fourth time, as she came to the end, someone said, "She's better than the little runt, anyway."

Noah Bugg was standing there, grinning and looking at Theo, who had just fallen at the end of the slide.

Noah sang out, "Greengrass, Greengrass, why don't you grow?" There was a sly smirk on his face. He sang it again, louder, and as Theo got up and came toward Poll, several other boys took up the chant. *Greengrass, why don't you grow* . . .

Poll said, "I wouldn't stand for that." Theo turned away, shrugging his shoulders, but she had seen his mouth start to tremble. She shouted at Noah, "You

60

skinny bully, you *caterpillar*," and charged him, head down. She hit him in the stomach; he grunted and fell and she fell on top of him. He tried to get up but she grabbed his hair with both hands and thumped his head up and down. He put his hand under her chin, pushing her off him, rolled her over, and held her flat on the ice. Slush trickled down her neck; she could feel it soaking through her clothes. She couldn't move but Noah's laughing face was above her so she spat into it as hard as she could and said, "Damn you, you rotten *bug,* damn and blast you to hell—"

Someone said, "Noah!" and the grin went from his face as if a curtain had fallen and covered it. He got up awkwardly and shuffled to the side of the pond, red hands dangling.

Aunt Sarah said, "Get up, Poll. It's time you went home, I think."

She waited, calm and aloof as a statue, while Poll scrambled up. Most of the boys seemed to have melted away; the few that were left stood in a group at the end of the slide, watching in silence. They were all scared of Aunt Sarah, Poll thought, and no wonder! There was something frightening about a person who never scolded, never even seemed to get angry, but who could make you feel just by the tone of her voice that you really had behaved very badly. "Get up, Poll," as Aunt Sarah said it, was worse than several hours of Aunt Harriet's nagging!

Aunt Sarah said nothing else all the way home.

Theo didn't speak either until they were in the house and Aunt Sarah had gone through to the kitchen. Then he caught Poll by the arm, turned her to face him, and whispered softly and savagely, "If you don't mind, I'll fight my own battles in future."

He marched upstairs and his bedroom door slammed. Poll would have liked to run and hide and cry privately but she was too wet and shivery. She gulped down the tears in her throat, lifted her chin, and went to the kitchen where Mother had a good fire and water heating up ready. She gave Poll a look and said to Aunt Sarah, "I thought someone might need a bath!"

Aunt Sarah said, "Poll has inherited one thing at least from our side of the family—Harriet's temper!" Her smooth face was serious but there was a smile in her voice. She said, "Get those wet clothes off at once, Poll."

The hip bath from the back of Poll's bedroom door was in front of the fire and a screen, made of thick cotton and stuck all over with picture postcards, stood round it to keep off the drafts. Poll's skin was red and stinging in patches with the cold slush that had seeped through her clothes, but after a minute or two in the lovely hot water she felt very comfortable and began to enjoy sitting in the little house the screen made, with the fire in front, the smell of bread cooking in the oven beside it, and the murmur of voices as Mother and Aunt Sarah sat talking over their tea. One of the postcards on the screen was a yellowing photograph of a fat old woman sitting on a donkey that Father and Mother had sent to Aunt Sarah when they went to Yarmouth on their honeymoon, and another, a colored picture of Niagara Falls that had come from Uncle Edmund when he first went on his travels. All the Gaiety Girls were there, and Dan Leno, a comic face with fuzzy, gummed-on hair, but Poll's favorite was a Christmas card of a snow-covered house, the roof sprinkled with frosting that sparkled beautifully in the light from the fire. The house had a paper front door that opened to show a red-carpeted hall with holly and a lit tree. Poll opened and closed the door and thought of Theo, who had warned her not to do that too often in case it came off, and wondered if he was still angry with her. It didn't seem fair if he was, she had only been taking his part, but nothing about Theo was simple.

She said, "Mother, you know that gold Dad brought home for us to make Christmas cards with? Is it valuable?"

There was a little pause. Mother and Aunt Sarah had been talking and Poll had broken into their conversation. Mother said, with a laugh, "Of course, Poll. All gold is valuable."

"Even tiny bits?"

"You know how small a gold sovereign is!"

Poll was pleased with this answer because it proved Theo was right. She would tell him so as a sort of peace offering and they could be friends again without her having to say she was sorry. She slipped low in the water and felt very settled and happy.

Mother was saying, ". . . when all's said and done, you can't help but be sorry. Poor Old Rowland, he set so much store by that boy of his! A mistake to have only one child, all your eggs in one basket, and he admits that he'd spoiled him. Apparently there had been trouble before, though not on this scale. Just petty pilfering when he was no more than a bit of a lad, nothing serious."

"If Mr. Rowland thought that, then he made a rod for his own back and I've no sympathy for him," Aunt Sarah said. "Stealing is always wrong, even if it is only a sweet or a hairpin, and no child is too young to understand that. A lesson learned young is a lesson for life! I hope you agree with me, Emily."

"Yes, Sarah. Of course." Mother's voice sounded humble but, when she came round the screen to open the oven door, her face didn't look it. She was smiling and her eyes danced as she tapped the bread with her knuckles to see if it was done.

The loaves rang with a hollow sound. Poll saw that one of them had run over the edge of its tin. "Please, Mother, can I have run-over and butter?"

Aunt Sarah said, "New bread is indigestible. Very bad for children."

Mother winked at Poll and held up a warm towel. Poll got out of the bath. Mother dried her, pulled her nightgown over her head, and put an old shawl round her shoulders. She folded the screen and Aunt Sarah helped her lift the bath and pour the water away down the sink in the scullery.

Aunt Sarah said, "I'm glad Mr. Rowland came, anyway. It showed respect for James."

"That wasn't his only reason for coming." Mother put the bath on the floor of the scullery and wiped it out energetically. She straightened up, very pink in the face. "He asked me if I was in need of money. Of course I said no."

Aunt Sarah didn't answer for several minutes. Mother went on polishing the inside of the hip bath and Aunt Sarah put on her outdoor clothes. She finished smoothing her gloves on and then said, speaking quickly and a bit breathlessly as if she felt she should have said this at once and not waited, "Yes, of course. There is no reason why he should help."

"Except that it's hard on you, having to pay for my pride?"

Mother came into the kitchen, eyes on Aunt Sarah, and Aunt Sarah smiled at her, not her normal pained and dutiful smile but an open and happy one that made her look very much younger and prettier. She said, "Nonsense, Emily dear," and kissed Mother's cheek.

When she had gone, Poll said, "Why didn't Aunt Sarah ever get married?"

"Too much sense."

"Don't be silly. I mean, *really.*"

Mother cut the crisp, run-over bread from the side of the tin, spread it with butter and gave it to Poll. "Well, it's true in a way. You won't find many women clever as Sarah in a long day's march and even fewer men. If you did find one who measured up to her, I daresay she'd frighten him off! But that's not the whole of it. Sarah had only just started teaching when Granny Greengrass got paralyzed and Sarah had to look after her as well as putting in long hours at school. And Mrs. Greengrass was a lot of work, let me tell you, a huge, big woman, going on for six foot and nearly as wide and with a voice like a gong. She ruled the house from her bed—you could hear her from the end of the street, shouting out orders! But it was Sarah who carried them out, kept the house going, saw her young brothers through school. So what chance had she to get married? They needed her money. There was nothing much else coming in except what Harriet got, pupil-teaching, which wasn't enough to feed a bird, really. Not that Sarah minded, mark you! She said it was her duty and pleasure to care for her mother, who'd worked hard enough in her time. Old Granny Greengrass had been chief pastry cook at the baker's and a bit of a slave driver to those under her, but she drove herself, too. Worked hard and died hard, people said."

"How old were you when her finger got chopped off?"

"Oh, just a little thing. But I heard about it, of

course, and when she died it got me into a nice bit of trouble. Did I never tell you that tale?" Mother looked at Poll and, when Poll shook her head, sat down on the other side of the fire. "Well, let me see, Sarah was about twenty-six then, so I'd be going on twelve. Old enough to know better, anyway. My mother had been helping Sarah with the old lady—there's always a lot of work at a deathbed—and when I came along to the house after school they were sitting down with a cup of tea in the parlor. So, seeing the coast clear, I nipped upstairs. I'd never managed to get a good look at that chopped-off finger and I thought, now's my chance! But I'd never seen anyone dead before either, and when I pulled the sheet back I got more than I bargained for. Her face was quite peaceful but when I touched her she was cold and stiff as a board and that scared me! I left her uncovered and ran down into the garden and stayed there until it began to get dark. Then I went in as if nothing had happened. I don't know where Mother was, but Sarah was sewing in the kitchen. She said, 'Have you been upstairs, Emily?' I said, 'No.' She asked me again, 'Are you quite sure?' and when I said yes, she gave me a straight look and went back to her sewing. I thought I'd creep out, but as I was going she said, 'Emily, would you go and get my silver thimble? I left it upstairs on the chest in the front room.' Well, that was where old Mrs. Greengrass lay dead, and it was dark now. I thought I would die of fright, but I was no match for Sarah, and upstairs I went."

Poll felt her skin creep. "That was mean of Aunt Sarah."

"Not really. I only had to tell her the truth and she would have let me off, but since I had stuck to my lie I had to be punished. You know your Aunt Sarah! She'd die rather than do a wrong thing herself and she expects the same standards in others. A bit hard to live up to, but we'll all have to do our best, living next door and under her eye." She looked at Poll grimly. "What made you get in a fight?"

Poll was taken aback; she had thought that was forgotten. "What did Aunt Sarah say?"

"Just you'd been scrapping but you'd been provoked."

"They laughed at Theo." Poll flushed with anger. "That Noah Bugg! He called him a runt!"

Mother sighed.

"Will Theo ever grow, do you think? It makes him so miserable."

Mother said, "If that's the only cross he ever has to bear in his life, he'll be lucky," and although she often made forbidding remarks of this kind, meaning nothing much by them, Poll felt scared suddenly. Perhaps it was the thought of a little girl being sent up, in the dark, to where a dead woman was lying, or perhaps it was just the growing dark in the kitchen, but it seemed to Poll, as her mother got up to light the oil lamp, that the world was full of unknown dangers, shapeless but menacing, like the shadows in the corners of the room.

4

A week passed—and something much worse did happen to Theo than being teased by Noah Bugg. Aunt Sarah knitted him a pink woollen vest and he had to wear it to school.

It was made of thick, soft wool and knitted in a pretty, lacy pattern. Mother said, "Sarah must have sat up till all hours; it is good of her. She says she'll have another one ready time this one needs to be washed." She saw Theo's sickly grin and added in a coaxing voice, "Your Aunt Sarah is worried about you getting a chill, this bitter cold weather."

"I'd rather get a chill than wear that," Theo said. "It's a girl's vest. I'd rather die."

He meant it; he felt really desperate. Mocking laughter filled his dreams; tormenting boys danced round him, gimlet eyed. *We can see what you're wearing,*

Baby Theo Greengrass! He prayed for a miracle—for the house to burn down and the hateful vest with it while they were all safely out—but his prayers were not answered. The first day of school, the humiliating garment was laid out on the chair at the end of his bed. He put it on and came down to breakfast wishing the earth would open and swallow him.

Poll tried to comfort him. "No one will see the vest under your clothes. No one will know."

"I'll know!" He pushed the porridge round his plate, the tears springing.

Mother looked at him helplessly. She said, "Sarah's so good to us, Theo. I can't tell her you wouldn't wear it."

"All right, all *right*. I'm wearing the beastly thing, aren't I?" Tears fell into his uneaten porridge and Poll began to cry too, in sympathy.

Mother said, "Oh, you two!" She got up from the table, went to the scullery, and began to throw dirty pots into the sink, making more noise than seemed necessary.

George, off to school early, hitched his satchel up on his shoulder and said, "For heaven's sake, Theo, can't you see you're upsetting her? Don't be so childish."

"I *am* a child," Theo said, sullenly hiccuping, but George had already gone, and was calling back from the door, "Mother, the milkman's here."

She came out of the scullery, drying her hands and muttering under her breath. She forgot to pick up the blue and white jug from the table and when she reached the door, she called Poll to bring it.

The milkman was saying, ". . . so the old sow farrowed early. D'you want a peppermint pig, Mrs. Greengrass?"

Poll looked at him, thinking of sweets, but there was a real pig poking its snout out of the milkman's coat pocket. It was the tiniest pig she had ever seen. She touched its hard, little head and said, "What's a peppermint pig?"

"Not worth much," Mother said. "Only a token. Like a peppercorn rent. Almost nothing."

"Runt of the litter," the milkman added. "Too small for the sow to raise. He'd only get trampled on in the rush."

Mother took the pig from him and held it firmly while it kicked and squealed piercingly. She tipped it to look at its stomach and said, "Well, he seems strong enough. And even runts grow."

The milkman took the jug from Poll and went to his cart to ladle milk out of his churn.

"Oh," Poll said. "Oh, *Mother.*" She stroked the small, wriggling body. Stroked one way, its skin felt silky to touch; the other way, stiff little hairs prickled her fingers. He was a pale apricot color all over.

The milkman came back. Mother said, "Will you take a shilling?" and he nodded and grinned. Poll took the milk to the kitchen and flew upstairs for her mother's purse. "Theo," she shouted as she ran back downstairs, "look what we've got!"

An old pint beer mug stood on the dresser. Mother laughed suddenly and popped the pig in it. He made such a fearsome noise that they put their hands over their ears. Poll picked him out and said, "Whatever made you do that?"

"I just thought he would fit, and he did!"

Poll put him down and he scampered desperately round the kitchen, dainty feet skittering on slippery linoleum. He shot into the scullery and went to ground in the little hole under the boiler.

Mother said, "Leave him now, poor little fellow, he's scared to death. He'll settle down while you're at school."

Poll groaned tragically. "Must we go? Oh, I can't bear it, I can't bear to leave him."

"He'll be here when you come home dinner time," Mother said.

Poll counted the hours. Not just that day, but the next and the next, the thought of the baby pig, waiting at home, distracted her attention so she had no time left to be naughty; by the end of the first week, she had not once been rapped over the knuckles or stood in the corner. She made a best friend called Annie Dowsett, who was older than she was and who told her how babies were born. "The butcher comes and cuts you up the stomach with his carving knife," Annie said. "But don't tell your mother I told you." Poll didn't really believe this, because if it were true, women would never have more than one baby, but it was an interesting idea all the same and she began to feel she quite liked this new school. She even liked her teacher, Miss Armstrong, who had a long, mild, sheep's face, and was proud that her aunt was headmistress with her name on a brass plate on the outside of the building. Everyone was a little scared of Aunt Sarah but not of Aunt Harriet, who was called Miss Harry to her face and Old Harry behind her back, who romped in the playground with the little ones until her wispy hair came down under her hat, and always brought potatoes to school to bake in the stove for the children who lived too far away to go home for their dinner.

Even Theo was happier because of the pig. The excitement of its arrival carried him through the first day and, although after that the horrible shame of the pink, girlish vest hidden under his clothes still haunted him sleeping and waking, especially when he caught Noah Bugg's rolling, gooseberry eye in the classroom, he managed to live with it. No one, he told himself, was likely to fall upon him and tear his clothes off, and even if he was sometimes tormented because of his size, he was used to that, and it was a comfort to run home and pick up the pig and whisper in his floppy ear, "Peppermint pig, peppermint pig, I'm a peppermint *boy,* so there's two of us, runts in this family."

Mother called the pig Johnnie, saying (rather oddly the children thought) that he reminded her of her grandfather, and it wasn't long before he answered to his name, grunting and running whenever they called him. At night, he slept in the boiler hole on a straw bed; during the day he trotted busily round behind Mother or sat on the hearth rug staring thoughtfully into the fire.

Lily said, "You can't keep a pig indoors, Mother!"

"Oh, we had all sorts of animals in the house when I was young," Mother said. "Jackdaws, hedgehogs, newly hatched chicks. I remember times you couldn't get near our fire."

"But not *pigs*," Lily said.

"I can't see why not. You'd keep a dog, and a pig has more brains than a dog, let me tell you. If you mean pigs are dirty, that's just a matter of giving a pig a bad name to my mind. Why, our Johnnie was housebroken in a matter of days and with a good deal less trouble than *you* gave me, my girl!"

Poll giggled and Lily went pink.

Mother said, "Give a pig a chance to keep clean and he'll take it, which is more than you can say of some humans. You tell me now, does Johnnie smell?"

If he did, it was only of a mixture of bran and sweet milk, which was all he ate to begin with, although as he grew older, Mother boiled up small potatoes and added scraps from the table. She said there was no waste in a house with a pig and when the summer came they would go round the hedgerows and collect dandelions and sow thistles so he would have plenty of fresh food and grow strong and healthy. "What he eats is important," she said. "Pigs are a poor person's investment."

"What's investment?" Poll asked.

"Oh, nothing," Mother said quickly. "Never you mind."

Poll said, "We aren't poor." She thought of Annie Dowsett, who wore a woman's cut-down dress and cracked boots and was one of the children Aunt Harriet baked a potato for every day. She wondered if she should tell Mother what Annie had said about how babies were born and decided against it—children were not supposed to know that sort of thing. She said, "Annie Dowsett's poor."

"There are degrees," Mother said, speaking absently, and with the creased, worried look on her face that was often there now and that the children had come to recognize as a sign to keep quiet and not ask for anything.

Even letters from Father did not seem to cheer her up as they should have done. Uncle Edmund had left the fruit farm in California to run a saloon in Colorado, and Father had gone with him. The saloon belonged to a woman called Bertha Adams, and for some mysterious reason Uncle Edmund was calling himself Adams, too. "I don't like it," Mother said to Aunt Sarah. "It smells fishy to me."

"How can Colorado smell fishy?" George asked. "It's nowhere near the sea, is it?"

Aunt Sarah gave him a look and he went back to his reading.

"It seems the fruit farm didn't belong to Edmund after all," Mother said. "James says he was manager but there had been some trouble."

"I don't doubt that," Aunt Sarah said. "It's an old story, isn't it? What I don't understand is how James let himself be taken in. He knows Edmund! And whatever else you might say about James, he has a good head on his shoulders."

"And a hopeful heart in his breast," Mother said. "The two organs are often at war with each other."

She put Father's letter behind the clock on the mantelpiece, looked at her reflection in the mirror above it, and ran her hands through her short, crisp curls. "Well," she said. *"Well.* If James isn't going to make our fortune just yet, I had better do something about it."

She went to Mullen's shop in the Market Square, dressed in her best coat with the jet trimming and her best hat. When she came back she looked smaller than usual, and tired. Poll and Lily watched her as she unpinned her hat and took it off with a sigh.

Lily said, "Are you going to work at Mullen's, Mother?"

She shook her head and sat down by the fire. Johnnie came and leaned against her and she pulled his ears gently. She said, "There's my good pig."

Lily said indignantly, "Why not? He said he'd give you a job, didn't he?"

"He offered me one. He wanted me to take charge of the workroom, set me over Marigold Bugg. I didn't like that idea for a start, bound to make trouble, but that wasn't all in his mind. When we went into it, I saw what he meant to do. He didn't say so outright, but I know the old devil! He doesn't like Marigold—she hasn't the grit to stand up to him and, though she's a good worker, best cutter he's got, it makes him look down on her. Once he'd got me in to do the cutting and fitting, he'd get rid of her, and what would she do then, the poor creature? That great boy to care for, and her old father who'd be in the workhouse if she couldn't keep him, and not a soul in the world cares for her."

Poll said, "But you don't *like* Mrs. Bugg, Mother? You couldn't possibly like her!"

"Since she counts me her friend, that makes it worse, doesn't it? I'd be letting her down twice over if I took her place."

Lily said, "Poor Mother," and went over to hug her. Poll wished she had thought of doing that and sat feeling left out while Mother held Lily's hand against her cheek and smiled up at her.

"Oh, Lily," she said, "whatever Marigold is like now, we were girls together and I can't forget that. She wasn't so pursed-up then, she still had a bit of spunk in her. When we were apprentices, we lived in, you know, and old Mullen was mean about food. Many a time there was just spotted dick for dinner and we threw it out of the window for the hens to pick over and crept down the back stairs to the grocery to get bread and cheese from the young man on the counter. 'You'll have me hung,' he'd say, but he always stumped up and back we'd go to the workroom, aprons bulging. One time Marigold almost got caught. She came face to face with old Mullen and he said, 'What are you up to, Miss? What have you got in your apron?' I was behind her, nearly dying of fright, but Marigold stuck her nose in the air and said, 'I'm surprised at you, Mr. Mullen, asking a lady such an indelicate question,' and swept straight past him, oozing outrage and virtue! Oh, it doesn't sound so funny perhaps, but we had a good laugh over the look on his face, and it makes me sad to see the meek way she speaks to him now . . ."

She gave a long sigh, looking into the fire, and then her face twisted suddenly and she turned to Lily and said, almost desperately, "Remember, Lily, that's the worst thing about poverty! Not hunger or leaky boots, but the way it drains out your spirit! However things turn out, you must never let that happen to you. Promise me!"

Poll said, bewildered, "I would hate to be hungry," and her mother gasped and jumped up from her chair and put her arms round her, holding her so close and tight that Poll could feel her heart fluttering.

"Oh, my lamb, of course you're never going to be. Did I frighten you? That was stupid, there's nothing to be frightened of. Everything is going to be quite all right, you must believe me."

Lily laughed. "Poll knows Aunt Sarah wouldn't let

us starve. She's just acting up, you know what she is! Don't worry, Mother."

Poll heard her mother's stays creak as she drew a deep breath and released it slowly. She let Poll go, smiled at Lily, and said in a quiet, even voice, "Yes, of course, dear. Of course we all know that. I was just being silly."

She had a notice printed to send to old clients and stuck one in the window.

EMILY GREENGRASS

Begs respectfully to inform the Ladies of
this District that she has Commenced
DRESS AND MANTLE MAKING
and hopes, by strict personal attention,
to merit a share
of their Patronage and Support.
Having been sole manageress
of the Dressmaking Department
of a well-known local store
for a number of years,
she feels confident of giving satisfaction
to her Customers in all orders
entrusted to her.
A GOOD FIT AND LATEST STYLE
GUARANTEED.

No one answered or came for several days, and then one afternoon old Miss Mantripp, who lived in the cottage at the end of the terrace, knocked at the door and asked if Mother could make her a blouse out of some lace she had "put by" for a special occasion.

"It's very good lace, Mrs. Greengrass," she said. "The end of a bolt brought from Paris that Her Ladyship gave me. I would have made it up myself but my eyes are too bad now for delicate work. I hope you'll take good care of it."

Miss Mantripp was about four foot six inches tall and bent over so that she appeared even smaller. She was a retired lady's maid, living on a tiny pension her employer had given her, and the children thought she was an extraordinary person. If anyone spoke to her early in the day, when she was shaking her rug at the door, or shuffling along to the shops in an old coat and slippers, all she would ever say was, "Don't talk mornings," in a gruff, grumpy voice. But as soon as midday had struck she took off her shabby clothes, put on a black dress with pearl buttons, and sat in her window with the curtains drawn back, looking out at the square and waiting for visitors.

No one ever came. Miss Mantripp was quite alone in the world, Mother said, and when the old woman called that afternoon, bringing the lace, Mother greeted her in her gentlest voice and sat her down by the fire.

Miss Mantripp was wearing her black dress and a huge, ancient straw hat that was nibbled into small holes round the edges as if the mice had been at it. Standing behind her chair, Poll nudged Lily and giggled, but Mother froze them both still with a look.

The lace might have been good once but it was now just very old lace and rotten in places. Mother rolled it up carefully and said it would be a shame to cut into such lovely material but she had a good piece of gray washing silk upstairs and if Miss Mantripp would like a blouse she would only charge her a shilling to make it.

The old woman looked pleased. "That would be very nice, Mrs. Greengrass. To tell you the truth, I only brought you the lace because I thought you could do with the work, but it would really have broken my heart to see it cut into."

She beamed at them all very sweetly and graciously and Mother said, with a catch in her voice that was either held-back laughter or tears, "You're very kind, Miss Mantripp. Would you care to stay and have tea with us?"

"I wouldn't want to intrude, Mrs. Greengrass."

"It's no intrusion, Miss Mantripp. We would all be delighted."

Mother put the best damask cloth on the table, eggs to boil on the fire, and cut thin bread and butter. Miss Mantripp sat primly at table, huge hat bobbing slightly as she made polite coversation. "Have you settled in comfortably, Mrs. Greengrass? The cottages are very small, are they not? Although I suppose it depends what you're used to. After all the years I spent with Her Ladyship I find it most strange to have no indoor sanitation. The arrangements here are most upsetting to a refined person. Each outside privy backing onto the one that belongs to the cottage next door! I am sure that you find it as distressing as I do, Mrs. Greengrass?"

"Well," Mother began, smiling doubtfully. "I'm not really sure what you mean."

"People sitting back to back," Miss Mantripp explained in low, horrified tones. "Back to back—and NO RELATION!"

Theo, who was ladling eggs out of the saucepan, gave a strangled cry and dropped one. He said, "Oh, Mother, I'm sorry." His face was scarlet, not because of the dropped egg but with the struggle to prevent himself laughing.

Mother said, "Never mind, Theo. Johnnie will clear up the egg." Her voice was almost natural, but the wild smile she swept in Miss Mantripp's direction was not. She turned it into a gasping laugh and said, "So useful having a pig in the house! It saves so much bending."

Theo said, "I'll put another egg on to boil."

"No, thank you, Theo . . ." But he had already vanished into the scullery, closing the door after him. Mother said, "Drat the boy. Poll, go and tell him there's no need to bother. I don't really want an egg." Then, as Poll got down from the table, she added, "Make sure you tell him that, won't you?" speaking emphatically as if this was a very important message Poll had to deliver.

"Yes, I'll tell him," Poll said.

Theo was leaning against the wall in the larder, wiping his streaming eyes. "I thought I'd die laughing," he said. "I expect I *will* die, next time I sit on the privy! Of course *we* sit back to back with our aunts so I suppose she would think that wasn't so dreadful since they're our relations. Though I'm not sure it's not *worse*. Can you imagine Aunt Sarah . . . ?"

"Don't be rude," Poll said coldly.

Theo pulled a face. "I didn't start it . . . There's no more eggs in the bowl. Mother better have mine."

"She doesn't want one. She told me to tell you."

"But that's silly. It was me broke the egg. So it's only fair—"

Poll said, *"No."*

Theo looked at her. "What's up?"

She said slowly, "I don't think Mother would like that. You making a fuss over who was to have the last egg. I expect there aren't any more because she could only afford to buy half a dozen. But she wouldn't want Miss Mantripp to know that because *she* might feel bad, being a visitor."

Theo shrugged his shoulders. "If you say so. But it seems a bit daft. *She's* daft, isn't she? Going on like that about privies. At the *tea table!* I really don't think I can sit there eating an egg. She'll just start me off again, laughing."

"Don't be so mean!" Poll felt very sad suddenly, she wasn't sure why. A mixture of no more eggs in the larder and little Miss Mantripp being so funny and kind. "It was nice to bring that old lace along, even though it was rotten. It's awful to make fun of her."

"Hey!" Theo said. "Hey! What's got into you, all of a sudden?"

Saturday was market day. Mother had started on Miss Mantripp's blouse and was anxious to get it finished and out of the way before other customers came. "Although it would be a good thing for them to see I've got something to do," she said. "People are quicker to place orders if they know someone else has already done so. I think I shall sit sewing in the front room all morning, looking busy. Poll and Theo, you can go shopping. There's not much we need, just two loaves of bread and perhaps half a pound of butter from the market stall near the church. It's always nice and fresh there."

"We're out of eggs," Theo said.

"Are we? Well, eggs are dear just now. But you can have a penny for sweets."

Theo frowned. Poll said, "Can we take Johnnie? He loves market day."

The pig grunted, hearing his name, and trotted along at their heels as he always did behind Mother when she went shopping. In the baker's he sat patiently waiting while Poll bought the bread, and the baker came round the counter and patted him and said what a good pig he was, just like a dog. "He's better than any old *dog*," Poll said scornfully. "Pigs are more intelligent than dogs, that's a scientific fact," and the baker laughed and gave her a sticky bun, free.

She offered to share it with Theo but he shook his head. He hadn't spoken since they left home. Poll said, "Is your throat sore? Or has the cat got your tongue?"

She bought Cupid's Whispers with the penny, little flat, sugary sweets with rhymes written on them. Then they went to the dairy stall near the church. Poll asked for the butter while Theo stood, gazing at the things set out on display. Blocks of lovely yellow butter, oozing salty drops of water, round cheeses cut to show their creamy insides, pieces of bacon for boiling, a basket of big, brown, speckled eggs . . .

There was a faraway expression in Theo's eyes as if he were lost in some dream. He put out his hand and took one of the brown eggs and put it in his pocket. He looked at Poll and saw she was looking at him, eyes round and startled. Theo grinned foolishly and her hand flew to her mouth to stop herself giggling. Theo felt his face growing hot. The woman who kept the stall smiled at the two pretty, fair children and said, "Have you got all you want now?"

"Oh," Poll said. "Oh, yes, thank you." Then, in a loud, bustling voice like a scolding old woman, "Where's Johnnie got to? *There* you are, you troublesome pig! Come on, Theo, stir your lazy stumps. We haven't got all day, you know."

She set off at a great pace down the cobbled path

85

that led to the church, through the gate into the churchyard, not stopping until she reached the flat tombstone everyone in the town called the Soldier's Grave, although the inscription was too worn to show who was buried there. Poll sank down on the stone, puffing her cheeks out and fanning herself with her hand as Theo and Johnnie came up to her. "Well," she said, still acting her old woman part, "well, I never did! Really!"

"I feel quite faint," Theo said. "At least, I feel very peculiar."

"Then you better sit down. Be careful you don't sit on the egg though."

Theo sat down. He took the egg out of his pocket and stared at it as if it was the first egg he had seen in his life. "I really don't know why I did that," he said, and he sounded and looked so amazed that Poll started to laugh. He watched her for a minute and then began to laugh too. They swayed helplessly, clutching their stomachs, and Johnnie sat looking up at them, intelligent, slitty eyes twinkling.

Several people, passing through the churchyard, saw the two Greengrass children sitting side by side on the Soldier's Grave and laughing fit to burst with their pet pig watching them, head on one side, as if wondering what they were laughing at. Some smiled as if they wondered too, but only one person stopped. He had followed them from the square and was standing a little way off, hands in his pockets and a thoughtful look on his face. When Poll and Theo grew quieter, he sauntered forward, kicking a stone. It landed in a spurt of dust by Theo's right foot and Theo looked up.

"I doubt if your aunt would find it so funny," Noah Bugg said.

Poll and Theo sat silent.

Noah shook his head sadly, "Thievin'," he said. "Stealin' from a poor market woman. What's funny in that?"

"I don't know what you're talking about," Theo said.

Noah laughed. Rooks flew with clapping wings out of the dark trees above them and cawed overhead.

Poll and Theo looked at each other. Then at Noah. They saw that his pale green eyes had darker green flecks round the pupils and that his gingery eyebrows above them were curiously bushy and stiff, as if he were a grown man, not a boy.

Theo looked at his boots. "Just one egg."

"One or a dozen, what's the difference?" Noah asked as if he really wanted to know.

Theo scuffed his boots in the dust and Johnnie got up from his haunches as if he thought it was about time they went home.

Noah's gooseberry eyes gazed into distance. " 'Course, we *could* ask Miss Greengrass. I reckon that's the sort of question she'd find pretty interestin'."

Theo sighed.

"I mean, she took us in Sunday School last year.

Sometimes the Bible and sometimes what she called Morals. About tellin' lies and stealin' and that. Mind you, I don't know as she'd *like* it if I asked her, exactly. Not seeing as it was her own nephew." He looked at Theo, eyes bright and spiteful. "My mother says, your precious family thinks such a lot of themselves. A cut above other people!"

Theo lifted his head. "Tell my aunt, then. Go on, go ahead! Or I'll tell her myself. I don't care!"

He stood up, smiling calmly at Noah who took a step back, drawing those strange heavy eyebrows together. "Come on, Poll, time we were moving. You'll get a chill if we sit here much longer."

She shook her head dumbly. She was shivering, but not with the cold. All the things she had overheard or been told these last months, but had not paid much attention to or only half understood, had suddenly come together in her mind and made frightening sense. They were dependent on Aunt Sarah until Father came home, or made his fortune in America and sent money back, and so they had to be good. If they weren't, Aunt Sarah might decide not to keep them and they would have to go to the workhouse. And Aunt Sarah's standards of goodness were unusually high. She had said, *Stealing is always wrong, even a sweet or a hairpin . . .*

Poll said, "She'll care, Aunt Sarah will care, she *will*, Theo!"

He shook his head, frowning to warn her, make her see it would be all right if they brazened it out, that if Noah believed they weren't worried he would most likely do nothing. He was only tormenting; he'd be far too scared of Aunt Sarah to go sneaking to her . . .

But Poll was scared *now*. She burst out, "Oh, please. Please, Theo, do stop him."

He looked at her, not understanding her terror but impressed all the same. Poll was frightened—*Poll*, who was so much braver than he was about almost everything! It made him feel old and protective. Of course, there was one way to settle the matter. If only he were bigger—or not quite such a coward! He hesitated, measuring himself against Noah, and knew that even if he could screw up his courage to impossible limits the fight would be over in seconds. Noah was only a few months older than he was but it might just as well have been years; he was a child beside this strong, well-grown boy!

He said, resigned, "Look, I'll put the egg *back*. Will that do? If you like, I'll tell the woman I'm sorry."

Noah shrugged his shoulders and grinned.

Poll jumped up from the Soldier's Grave and pleaded with him. "Don't tell Aunt Sarah, please, Noah."

"Worth a lot, is it? Well, it depends . . ."

His green eyes narrowed, sharp as flints, and she shrank against Theo.

He said, "Leave her alone, Noah; she's only a girl, no need to bully her." Then, to Poll, "I'll see to this. You go on. I'll catch up when I'm ready."

89

There was a note of command in his voice she had not heard before. She picked up the shopping basket, retreated as far as the churchyard gate, Johnnie trotting beside her, and stood looking back. The boys were out of earshot but she could see that Theo was doing all the talking, waving his hands about energetically, and that Noah was listening with a surprised but interested expression. She took a Cupid's Whisper out of her pocket, reading the rhyme before she ate it. "Cherry Ripe, With lips so red, With curls so bright, You'll soon be wed." Sucking the sweet, she crouched down and put one arm round Johnnie's neck for additional comfort, hugging his warm, solid body and thinking, with part of her mind, that it was amazing how fast he seemed to be growing. Much too big for the boiler hole now, he would soon be too big to be allowed indoors all the time. Mother complained that he got under her feet sometimes in the kitchen and said that when the weather got warmer she would make up a bed for him in the old hen house at the end of the garden. Poll rubbed her chin against the bristly hairs of his neck and sighed, "Oh, poor Johnnie."

It seemed that ages passed, but it was only five minutes by the church clock when Noah nodded at Theo and walked away and Theo came slowly toward her.

He was pale faced but smiling.

Poll was relieved by the smile. "He won't tell?"

"No, I've fixed that. But really, Poll, you *are* a

dimwit! You should never give in to a blackmailer!" His smile grew broader and the color came back into his cheeks. "Lucky he's a pretty stupid one!"

"What d'you mean?"

"Nothing."

"You must have meant something."

"Well . . . perhaps. Let's say it's nothing you need to know about, anyway. Just that you needn't be scared anymore because I've found a way of stopping his mouth that won't cost me anything though *he* thinks that it will." He looked at Poll, eyes shining with secrets and a faint hint of malice. "It's a bit subtle for you, I'm afraid. You might not understand if I told you."

And he wouldn't tell her. Even though she persisted, all the way home and for several days after until she grew tired of asking, all he would ever say was, "It's best you shouldn't know. Safer, really. It's between me and Noah, so you leave it like that and just trust me."

5

By the time Easter came Poll felt she had lived in Norfolk for years and knew every inch of the town, not like a real map with contours and rivers, but like a private one, drawn in her mind. If she closed her eyes she could see a dancing bear in the Market Square, Theo and Noah in the churchyard, a robin's nest among the primroses in the bank down Tank Lane, herself skipping with her new rope down the avenue of walnut trees at the back of the church or turning somersaults on the white wooden railings of the Town Pit and hanging up-side down to watch the shire horses standing to drink, lifting their great, dripping mouths . . .

"Why the Town *Pit?*" she asked. "It's a pond."

"Ponds are always called pits in Norfolk," Aunt Sarah said.

"I saw an elephant bathe in the Town Pit once when the circus came," Aunt Harriet said. "That was a sight and a half! Everyone standing round in their best clothes after church and all of them soaked to the skin when he rolled over and blew from his trunk. And Eel's Pit is where we went skating, of course, and Bride's Pit is a good place for frog's spawn."

"Not a place to go after dark," Mother said. "Have I told you *that* dreadful tale? How the pit got its name? One night, long ago, a bride and groom drove out of the town in a closed coach drawn by two fine black horses. It was a wild night, clouds blowing over the moon, and when the coachman came to Bride's Pit he missed the road and turned down the cart track instead, into the water. He tried to turn back but too late. The coach was too heavy to turn and they all vanished forever, the coachman, the horses, the poor young couple cut off in their prime. On dark nights, they say, you can hear it all happen again, the wheels of the coach on the road, the galloping horses, the terrible screams of the bride . . ."

"Just a tale," Aunt Sarah said. "I think it was called Bird's Pit originally because there were a lot of birds nesting there, and the name changed over the years, as names do."

"Annie Dowsett lives on the road past Bride's Pit," Poll said. "I wouldn't like to be her, going home wintertime."

"Don't you spend too much time with that Annie Dowsett," Mother said.

"Why not?"

"Just because."

"Annie's my friend," Poll said, but under her breath and so softly that only Theo heard her.

Poll knew quite well why her mother disliked Annie Dowsett, because she liked her for just the same reason. Annie was rough, she wore old clothes all the time, she fought with boys and was ready for anything. She even agreed to accompany Poll into the slummy part of the town, called the Shambles, a tightly packed jumble of narrow streets and old houses that Aunt Sarah said no nicely brought up girl would walk through, even in daylight, and certainly not after dark. "I'd be scared," Lily said, with a shudder, and so, naturally, Poll wanted to go there.

She and Annie went into the Shambles the last day of the Easter term, after school. Poll was nervous at first, not knowing what to expect, and then disappointed to find nothing really alarming, only a rather dirty place where vegetable rubbish squelched underfoot and women stood on their doorsteps and gossiped while their babies played round their feet.

Poll thought she had never seen so many babies, fat ones and thin ones, pale ones and rosy ones, crawling in the dirt, clinging to their mothers' skirts, or sitting, grubby and grumbling, in rickety prams. One baby stopped crying and smiled at her when she picked up his rattle from the ground where he'd thrown it. His fat cheeks were solid and shiny. Poll said to his mother,

"Look, he likes me. Can I take him for a walk, do you think?"

The woman looked at Poll without answering. She was tall and big in the chest with a dark, heavy face and hard, glistening eyes, like dark glass. When she started to laugh, throwing her head back, Poll saw that she had a lot of teeth missing and that one of those that were left was long and sharp, like a spike, or a fang. She stared, fascinated, and then realized that the woman was laughing at *her*. As she backed away, the woman on the next doorstep began laughing too, and the next woman and the next, until the cruel, raucous noise seemed to fill the whole street and press on her eardrums like thunder. Annie grabbed at her hand. "Come on," she said urgently, *"run . . ."*

They ran, mud splashing their legs—and worse things than mud, Poll thought, wrinkling her nose—through mean, twisting alleys, past dark, open-doored hovels and staring, slatternly women, to the safety of the wide Market Square. They filled their lungs with clean air and looked at each other, Poll sheepishly, Annie astonished. "Whyever d'you want to speak to her for? Bit daft, warn't it?"

"I don't know." Poll felt sick with shame. That horrible, jeering laughter still rang in her head.

"Lucky she warn't drunk, or she might've clobbered you one for your cheek," Annie said.

"I only asked to take her baby out, didn't I? That wasn't rude!"

"Bit queer-like, though. I spec' she thought you was mental."

"Don't see why. I like playing with babies. And we haven't any at home, in our family."

Annie shrugged. "If you want babies, you c'n come to my house and welcome, any time you've a mind to."

"Thank you," Poll said. "I'd like to sometime. I'll ask my mother." She hoped it didn't show in her face that she knew Mother would never give her permission.

In fact she went without it, only two days later and in a howling temper.

That was the Thursday before Easter. After midday dinner, Mother made her first batch of hot cross buns, working the yeasty dough with floury hands, marking the little brown cakes with the back of a knife, and setting them to rise in front of the fire. She went into the scullery to wash the bowl and her hands—turning her back for barely a minute—and when she came back the buns had all gone. Not a crumb left, only a plumpy, satisfied pig, sitting square on the rag rug and smiling into the fire.

"Drat that animal!" she said, and reached for the broom. "Hen house for you!"

Poll heard Johnnie squeal and ran to the kitchen. George, who had been sitting reading at the table, looked up and said calmly, "Not his fault, Mother. How was the poor fellow to know?"

"You couldn't have stopped him, I suppose? Nose in a book as usual."

"Not a crime, is it?"

"Not much help, let's say. And I've got enough to do without pampering pigs! Miss Duval's dress to finish, now this! I'm just about at the end of my tether!"

"Hot and cross like your own buns, in fact," George observed to the air.

This silly joke didn't help matters. Mother set her lips ominously, jabbed at Johnnie's behind with the broom, and drove him, grunting, into the garden and down the long cinder path. Poll followed to the hen house, protesting, "It's not fair to shut him up, Mother."

"Fair or not, that's where he's going and that's where he'll stay."

"He didn't mean to do anything wrong. The buns were where he could reach them. Perhaps he thought they were meant for him, as a treat."

"My fault, I suppose? Oh, well, that's one good lesson learned! Ridiculous, letting a great pig have the run of the house. A pig is a pig and he'll be treated like one from now on."

"But he's not used to it, he's used to being a *person.*"

Johnnie stood inside the hen run, ears flopping forward over his eyes, looking up with what seemed to Poll a dejected expression.

"He's hurt," she said. "His *feelings* are hurt. How'd you feel if you'd always been petted and allowed in by the fire and you were driven out suddenly and locked up in prison? Oh, it's wicked and cruel! *You're* cruel, Mother!"

"That's enough from you, my girl."

"I hate you," Poll said.

Mother looked at her levelly. "I didn't hear that."

And Poll did not dare repeat it. Not to her face, anyway. Nor did she dare to let Johnnie out, although, when her mother had gone back indoors, she examined the gate of the hen house and was glad to see the catch was so rotten that he only had to give one good push in the right place to set himself free. She scratched his back to console him, and whispered, "Poor Johnnie, you *good* pig, she's hateful! *I* hate her, I hate her so much I'll never forgive her for this as long as I live."

She meant it. Hatred swelled inside her like a balloon, as if it might burst her chest open. She wished she could go right away and never see or speak to her mother ever again. Dad had gone, hadn't he? Now she saw why! He couldn't bear to stay with such a mean, spiteful person. Where could *she* go? Well, one place for a start. She said, in a voice hoarse with tears, "I'm going off to see Annie, that's where I'm going, and I may never come back."

And she set off at once on what was to be, by the end of the day, the most frightening journey she had ever made in her life.

Only Miss Mantripp saw her go. Sitting in her window, proudly wearing her new blouse and waiting for visitors, she smiled at the youngest Greengrass girl running by and said to her pet thrush, a fat bird called Kruger who was the only living creature she spoke to, most days, "There's that sweet, pretty child."

Poll didn't notice her. Burning eyes fixed on the road, she ran as if there were devils behind her until she was well clear of the town, out of breath, and feeling better for it. She had run off her temper and when she reached the old road mender, sitting by his pile of stones on the grass verge, she called out, "Afternoon, Mister, how's the work going?" and smiled gleefully, knowing what his answer would be because it was always the same.

And she was right. He pushed up the dark glasses he wore to protect his eyes from flying flints and said slowly, "Waaal, thaaart be a mucky rumman." It seemed that these six words were the only ones he knew, and Aunt Harriet said that no one really understood what he meant by them because he used them on every occasion; for instance, if it rained, he would look up at the sky, put a sack over his head, and announce, "Waaal, thaaart be a mucky rumman."

Poll laughed and skipped on, staying in the middle of the road because the deep ruts at the side wore your boots out, but keeping a sharp eye on the hedgerows. There were birds' nests to watch for, and perhaps she might see a weasel with her babies running behind her nose to tail, for all the world (so Aunt Harriet said) like a string of circus elephants, only smaller, of course. No such luck today; just a cock pheasant, whirring up from the other side of the hedge with a clatter of wings and a spine-chilling yell, just before she came to Bride's Pit . . .

Lucky to get away, that old pheasant, she thought, because there was a Gypsy camp at the pit, two painted caravans parked on the green cart track the bride's coach had plunged down into the water, washing spread out on the bushes and cooking pot steaming. Barking dogs hurled themselves the length of their chains as Poll passed, but the Gypsies only stared at her, bold eyed and unsmiling. She didn't have the courage to linger although she'd have liked to—it seemed such an enviable life, meals out-of-doors and no school, and it would have been exciting to get more than a glimpse of the inside of one of those caravans. What she could see, gleaming brass and bright curtains, looked invitingly cosy and comfortable.

By contrast, Annie's house seemed a poor, gloomy place: a tiny thatched cottage, some centuries old, crouching in the shadow of a densely overgrown wood. As Poll left the sunny road and walked up the short, muddy track, the air seemed to grow perceptibly damper and chillier and if Annie had not been there, at the open front door, she might have lost her nerve and turned back. Annie said, "I didn't think you'd come, really," and ran indoors, leaving Poll standing there, feeling awkward, until Annie's mother appeared, one baby straddling her hip, another peeping out from behind her. She looked more like Annie's grandmother than her mother, Poll thought, with her scraped-back hair and sad eyes set in deep hollows, but her thin face was friendly when she smiled and invited Poll in.

There was only one room downstairs and, although the stone floor was swept and clean and there were pots of geraniums on the windowsill, there was very little furniture in it: a table, a few stools, a wheelback chair by the fire, and an old sack instead of a hearth rug. No books, no pictures, no friendly clutter of ornaments! This seemed strange to Poll, almost alarming. Surely even very poor people had things in their houses they liked to look at? Thinking this, she was half afraid to look at Annie, but when she did Annie just grinned at her and said, to her mother, "Poll likes babies."

She could not have sounded more disbelieving if she had said, "Poll likes saber-toothed tigers."

Her mother said, "It's just as well we're not all like you, Annie, or it 'ud be a poor lookout for the human race. Here you are, Polly." She put the baby who was perched on her hip into Poll's arms and shook her head when he started to whimper and fight to get back to her. "I'd be right glad to be free of him for a while, I can tell you. On the grizzle ever since he woke up this morning, poor little tinker. Annie, you take our Archie too, and stay out till teatime."

Archie was three years old, pink cheeked and

bright eyed and solid as a little rock. Poll's baby, Tom, was about a year younger and very much quieter; after a minute or two he seemed content to be carried by this strange girl, and settled with his head on her shoulder and his thumb in his mouth.

"Like to see our pig?" Annie said.

Poll said she would, but regretted it. The Dowsett pig stood knee-deep in filth in a ramshackle sty surrounded by nettles. Some pigs have mean, narrow faces but his was friendly and blunt and his flat, damp nose turned up at the tip, giving him an engaging air of comic surprise. Poll scratched his back pityingly and thought of Johnnie, scrubbed every few days with the garden broom and kept, Mother said, pink and sweet as a clean baby's bottom. She asked, "What's his name?"

"Just Pig," Annie said. "What's the point, givin' a name to a pig what's going to be killed come the autumn?" She gave a wild snort of laughter. "Our last pig didn't 'alf holler!"

Poll felt dizzy with shock. She said faintly, "Our pig's called Johnnie."

Annie looked at her sidelong. "Oh, well," she said, after a minute. "Your pig's a special pig, like. That's a bit different."

They took the babies through a meadow to a shallow brook that chuckled between sandy banks. Archie splashed at the edge of the water, shouting with laughter. Poll put little Tom down on the grass and tickled his stomach to make him laugh too, but although he smiled once or twice he soon started to whine and chew at his knuckles and seemed happier when she sat quiet and he could nestle against her. He felt hot and Poll dipped her hankerchief in the cool water and bathed his head with it. Annie called him a "miserable little bugger" but Poll enjoyed comforting him and, while Archie and Annie ran races and threw stones in the river, she rocked Tom and sang to him until Annie said it was time to go back.

Poll had not meant to stay for tea. The Dowsetts were too poor to want to feed visitors. But the table was laid and Annie's mother had set a place for her. They had boiled bacon pudding and bread spread with dripping flavored with rosemary that tasted so good Poll ate four thick slices. When she had finished, Tom climbed onto her lap and went to sleep there. Mrs. Dowsett said, "You've got a good way with babies, I can see that with half an eye."

Poll beamed proudly. She would have liked to stay in the warm, smoky cottage, cuddling Tom while he slept, but dusk was falling outside, bats flitting against the dark wood. She said, reluctantly, "I ought to go home."

"Annie'll show you a piece of the way," Mrs. Dowsett said. "There's a shortcut, no need to traipse all the way back by the road."

They went round the back of the cottage, skirting the wood, to a path through the trees. Annie said, "Turn right at the end, you can't miss."

It looked very gloomy, gloomy and secret. No bird song, no rustles. Only the squeak of their boots on damp grass.

Poll said, "Is it far?"

Annie shook her head. She seemed unwilling to stay any longer and Poll was ashamed to admit she would rather go home by the road. She said good-bye as cheerfully as she could manage and set off down the green, grassy way.

Purple shadows around her. Above, a thin strip of navy blue sky with no stars. Poll hummed softly to keep her courage up. She wasn't afraid—there was nothing to be afraid of, in a wood, and she couldn't get lost as long as she kept to the path. But which path? She came to a fork. Was it here she had to turn right? She decided to keep on what seemed the main track, but quite soon it started to narrow and the branches closed over her head. Should she go back? Was this the way through the wood or only a poacher's trail? Poll thought of poachers and her heart thudded. She thought, *mantraps!* There was an old mantrap hanging outside Nero's junk shop in Station Street, a hideous iron contraption with cruel teeth and a notice above it that said NERO'S LITTLE NIPPER. Aunt Harriet said it was just an old curiosity and that mantraps were illegal now, but how could she be sure there was not one left in this wood, abandoned and rusty but savagely dangerous still? Poll walked on delicately, straining to see where she put her feet down and, when the path widenened again, held her breath and ran down the center of it until the trees began to thin out and she came to a road.

She breathed easier out of the wood but the road was not one she knew. She turned right, came to a fork, hesitated, and turned right again. Although the moon had risen now and was bobbing along beside her on the other side of the hedgerow, a wind had got up and ragged clouds blew across it. Poll trudged on with aching legs and sinking heart as the night became wilder and blacker. When she saw a tiny light some way off the road, she laughed aloud with relief and broke into a run.

The light flickered in the upstairs window of a cottage at the end of a farm track. The garden gate creaked as Poll opened it, startling her. She expected a dog to bark but there was no sound except the wind in the tall trees overhead as she pushed her way through a tangle of brambly bushes to the cottage door. She knocked timidly, waited, and then knocked again, harder. No one answered. She stepped back and called up to the window. "Please! Is anyone there?"

A long time seemed to pass. The silence unnerved her. Who lived here, in this lonely place? An old witch perhaps! Should she just creep away? Then curtains were drawn back with a rattle of wooden rings and a head appeared, silhouetted against the pale, yellow light. An old man with white hair.

"Please," Poll said. "Please. I'm sorry. I'm lost!"

The old man peered down at her. "Whar d'yew

want to git to?" he asked, and, when she told him, gave a high, thin, rattling, laugh that turned into a cough, breath wheezing in and out as if his chest was a dusty bellows. When he could speak again, he said hoarsely, "Ah, thaart's a fair traipse from hare, Mawther. Ah've not bin thar this ten year, a rare old traipse, like, but if yew kips on the road thaart'away, yew'll git thar afore the night's done."

He spoke in broad Norfolk, like the old roadman, but Poll understood him—"mawther" meant girl or woman—and he was clearly pointing in the direction she was already going. She thanked him politely, feeling a good deal less weary now she knew she was on the right way, and when she got back to the road, hopped and skipped along eagerly, beginning to enjoy what suddenly seemed an adventure, out on her own, this wild night! Theo would have been afraid, but she wasn't. How she would boast when she got home! That funny old man!

The wind lifted her hair from her scalp and blew her along like a leaf or a bird. She was flying before it. She cried, "On the road thaart'away, Mawther, yew'll git thar afore the night's done."

She had not really been lost; she knew where she was now! Just ahead was a familiar bend, and beyond the bend lay Bride's Pit. She slowed down a little and tried to walk quietly. Once she was past, safe past the bend and the pit, she would run the last mile . . .

Then she heard it! Heard galloping horses, and,

above the drumming sound of their hooves, the wheels of the coach. Terror seemed to drive the breath from her body but she walked on mechanically, hypnotized by what she knew she would see when she turned the next corner.

And see it she did. First Bride's Pit. The Gypsies had gone and it looked very desolate, the water velvety black against the gray grass. Then the phantom coach with two galloping horses coming toward her, a coachman on the box and carriage lamps lighting the hedgerows. Poll stopped and shrank into a gateway, waiting for what was going to happen: for the horses to turn off the road down the cart track and for the terrible screams that must follow as they plunged into the pit.

She opened her mouth to scream herself but no sound came out. The coach was so close now she could see sparks flying from the hooves of the horses and the pale gleam of the coachman's face under his hat. Her legs gave way beneath her and she sank to her knees, covering her eyes with her hands.

The ground shook; the iron sound of wheels deafened her. She froze to the ground like a hare as the coach passed Bride's Pit. Not a ghostly conveyance, but the mail coach that left the Market Square every night as the church clock struck nine! She looked up as it passed her, watched it sway round the bend, listened as the sound of wheels and hooves died away.

It was some time before she moved. She had never felt so cold in her life—nor so vulnerable. As if nothing would ever be safe and solid again. Although she had not in fact seen a ghost, she had met fear of a kind she had not known before. And that frightened her. Her own fear frightened her.

As she walked slowly homeward she tried to give this fear shapes—there was a donkey that haunted Tank Lane and a black dog local people had seen that was sometimes bad, sometimes good—but the thought of these friendly ghosts did not frighten her now. Nor ever would, ever again, she realized suddenly. The fear that walked with her was a dark dream in her mind and had no shape at all . . .

When she heard running footsteps approaching, *they* did not frighten her. She marched steadily on, head held high.

Theo had been running so fast he was wheezing. He gasped, "I thought you might come this way. Mother was in such a state! Then I remembered Annie and I guessed you'd gone there!" He giggled and wheezed like the old man at the cottage. "Teaching Mother a lesson!"

"She shut Johnnie up!" That seemed years ago.

"Silly ass." But he squeezed her hand fondly.

"Has she let him out?"

"Of course! You know Mother! Up in the air one minute . . ." He stopped. "She's pretty angry with you though."

Poll nodded, paying no heed to this warning. "I

was at Bride's Pit when the mail came. I thought it was the Bride's Coach."

"Oh, Poll! Were you scared?"

"Just a bit. Not for long though!"

He gave an excited groan. "I'd have *died.*"

"No, you wouldn't. It wasn't like that."

But she couldn't explain what it *was* like, couldn't find the right words. She was too tired, suddenly, longing for home, for the comfort of her mother's warm lap. Perhaps, as a special treat, Mother might give her a cup of hot elderflower wine with fingers of toast . . .

The front door stood open. She ran down the passage and threw open the door of the kitchen.

Mother and Aunt Harriet were standing there, waiting. There was no comfort in their expressions, no loving welcome. Their faces loomed over her, their voices rose. *"You naughty girl . . ."*

Poll closed her ears and her mind and let the waves of their anger break over her. When they seemed to have tired themselves out, she said calmly, "I'm all right, what's the fuss about?"

Mother let out her breath in a sigh and sat down. She looked sick and exhausted and Poll wanted to run to her but Aunt Harriet stood in the way. Her eyes glittered and her mouth was down at the corners. "Is that all you can say when your poor mother's been half out of her mind with the worry?"

Poll shrugged her shoulders. What could she say

with Aunt Harriet standing there between her and Mother? She muttered, "Not my fault if she's stupid."

Aunt Harriet's face was red as fire—as if she might breathe out flames and smoke in a minute! "You wicked child! If you're not ashamed of upsetting your mother, then think of Theo! Rushing out after you in this weather without his coat on and in his delicate health! Mark my words, if he catches his death, it'll be at your door!"

Mother said, half laughing, "That's enough, Harriet," and got up from her chair to come toward Poll, arms outstretched. But she was too late. Poll pushed her hands away, shouting, "Damn you, damn the whole blasted lot of you, damn you to hell!" and ran upstairs, weeping.

6

Theo came to no harm from that chilly spring night but Poll caught scarlet fever from little Tom Dowsett and nearly died of it.

She was so hot in church Easter Sunday. Her cream alpaca dress weighed her down, her starched knickers cut into her, and the elastic that held on her new floppy hat was a steel band under her chin. When they stood up for the hymn her legs bent like a rag doll's legs and she whispered to Lily, beside her, "I do feel so queer." But Lily was singing her heart out. She was in love with the Vicar, a handsome man with a wooden leg, and in church she saw and heard no one but him. Poll tried to sing but her throat hurt. The organ boomed in her hollow head and made her feel giddy. She looked up at the high roof of the church and it seemed that the carved wooden angels were flying above her, dipping and swooping like swallows. The next thing she knew, she was sitting outside the church on the Soldier's Grave, her mother's hand on the back of her neck and cold stone beneath her.

Then she was at home, in her bed, and the doctor leaned over her. He had a black, curly beard and his breath smelled of onions. She turned her head away while he examined her chest and her stomach but when he made her open her mouth so he could inspect her throat she got the full blast of his oniony breath. It made her sick and Mother cleaned her up and sprinkled her pillow with lavender water. The doctor stood by the window, huge body blocking the light, and Poll heard him say, "Hospital's the best place. I'll send the fever cart for her."

Poll screamed. Screamed and screamed, although the pain seemed to slice her throat open, until the doctor put his hands over his ears and her mother gathered her up in her arms, stroked her damp hair back, and said, "Hush, my lamb. D'you think I'd send you to any old hospital?"

She hung a sheet soaked in carbolic over Poll's door and put the tin bath just outside it so she could wash and change all her clothes whenever she left Poll to look after the others. For the first nightmarish days and nights that wasn't often; whenever Poll woke, her mother was there to change her nightdress and bathe her hot head. Sometimes Aunt Sarah sat with her but no one else came except Lily once, creeping in when Mother was busy downstairs, thinking Poll was asleep.

Poll was dreaming. She dreamed someone had kissed her, and when she opened her eyes she saw Lily there, lovely face serious, eyes wide and dark in the candlelight. Lily put her finger to her lips. "Don't make a sound, I shouldn't be here. Darling Poll, please get better."

It hurt Poll to talk. She croaked, "Go away, Lily. You'll catch scarlet fever."

"I don't care," Lily said nobly. She sat on the bed and took Poll's hot, sticky hand. She was wearing a new blouse and a high, stiff Eton collar.

Poll said, "That's a *boy's* collar!"

"Aunt Sarah made me wear it. She says it looks smart! *I* think it's hateful but you know what she is, she likes us to look different from other people." She sighed; her cool hand stroked Poll's. "Oh, Poll, I've just been to church and HE prayed for you."

"D'you mean the Vicar?"

Lily nodded and blushed. "He did it so beautifully. Everyone cried." Tears filled her own eyes at the memory. She gazed into distance, lips softly parted, and Poll knew she was dreaming that she was ill too and the Vicar was praying for *her*. All the congregation down on their knees and his sad eyes lifted to Heaven! Poll thought, *Lily wouldn't mind dying if it made him take notice of her!*

She wanted to laugh but it was too much of an effort. She whispered, "Aunt Harry says he takes his wooden leg off when he goes to bed and stands it up in the corner. Is it really Sunday again?"

"Yes. You've been ill a whole week. We've all been so frightened." Lily's tears trembled like pearls at the end of her lashes; one fell and rolled down her cheek. "Please, Poll, don't die. We all love you so much. Aunt Sarah's promised to buy me a bicycle if I pass my exams in the summer, and if you're a good girl and get better, I'll let you ride on it sometimes."

Poll cried when she'd gone. Not because Lily believed she might die but because her legs felt so weak she was sure she would never be able to ride Lily's bicycle. When Mother came in she saw her wet eyes and asked what was the matter but Poll couldn't tell her, just turned her head away and wept bitterly.

Perhaps those tears did her good. She slept properly for the first time, without frightening dreams, and when she woke up the fever had left her. She felt limp and tired but her bones had stopped aching and her head was comfortable on the soft pillow.

The night was almost over. The window showed pearly gray and outside there was a gentle, squeaky, insistent sound like the sound of birds waking up in the morning. The sleepy dawn chorus. And yet it wasn't quite that. She lay listening. Then said, "Mother!"

Her mother turned in her chair by the window. "Yes, my lamb?"

Poll said, "Listen."

The noises continued: a delicate squealing and chirping; a hushed sighing like a calm sea washing pebbles; a rustling and scattering; a low, mysterious whistle; a sweet, musical bleating . . .

"Sheep going by," Mother said. She wrapped Poll in a blanket and carried her to the window. Day was a pale lemon streak over the rooftops; below, in the square, the flock and the shepherds passed in blue shadow, iron hurdle wheels squeaking, dainty hooves pattering, baby lambs baaing, the dog at their heels giving low-pitched little yelps as if he did not want to disturb the slumbering town.

"I thought it was birds," Poll said when they had gone out of sight. "It sounded like birds."

Her mother put a hand on her forehead. She said, "You're cool now. You're better, aren't you?" Her voice was solemn but happy, full of a hushed, weeping joy. She put Poll back in her bed, smoothed her pillow, and smiled down at her. "Shall I make you some warm milk and honey?"

"No, thank you," Poll said. "I'm all right. You go to sleep. I want to listen to the morning."

Poll had to stay in her room for six weeks until the infection had left her. The world shrank to four walls and a window and what went on outside was a story she had no part in and could only listen to. Some of the things she heard were happy, some of them sad.

She heard the passing bell begin to toll. It would ring seven times for a man, six for a woman, three for a child. Poll lay in her bed, dreamily listening. ONE—a horse clattered by in the square. TWO. THREE—and the deep sound trembled on the air as if the bell were sorry to stop so soon. Four, five, six, the voice of death sang, but these last peals were only echoes. Mother came into her room and told her the Dowsett baby was dead. Not little Tom, but his bouncing three-year-old brother. Poll felt very strange, sad and excited at the same time. Poor Annie! She must feel so important, going to school and telling everyone her brother was dead! Archie, lying in his coffin, waxen face covered with flowers. Poll thought, *I might have died too,* and started to cry.

Mother said, "I must go to that poor woman. Shall I take your love to Annie? Do you think she'd like me to make her a dress?"

Most of the day now, Mother's treadle sewing machine whirred in the front room downstairs. She had plenty of customers but she found time to make a dress for Annie, a best dress with lace collar and cuffs and a tucked bodice. Poll said, "She'll want new boots, too. No use having a new dress and old boots."

"I'll see what I can manage," Mother said. "There's a pair Lily's grown out of she's hardly worn. They'd do for the summer."

"Is it summer already?" Poll said.

The year had turned while she was ill. With the first of the really warm weather, Miss Mantripp hung Kruger's cage in her cottage doorway and the thrush's liquid song poured in at Poll's window. She sat, propped up on pillows, cutting pictures out of magazines for her scrapbook. She stuck Father's postcards in, too. He had left Uncle Edmund and the saloon in Colorado and found a job as valet to a rich Englishman who was traveling round America. Since he heard Poll was ill, he had sent her a card almost every day, covered in such tiny writing it hurt her eyes to read it. The cards came from the Grand Canyon, from Niagara Falls, from San Francisco (Aunt Sarah said they would be useful for geography and bought Poll an atlas), but the card Poll liked best was made of soft leather with a picture of a bear on it and the message I CAN HARDLY BEAR TO LEAVE YOU. Once, Poll went to sleep with this card tucked under her cheek and the leather dye came off on her skin.

She wasn't bored. She had her scrapbook, and Aunt Harriet's collection of birds' eggs to look at, and a huge pile of Chatterbox Annuals, and Aunt Sarah's photograph album, a heavy, leather-bound volume with a brass clasp. "All your ancestors, dear, that should interest you," Aunt Sarah said, and there they all were: whiskered gentlemen and crinolined ladies sitting beside potted palms; Granny Greengrass was there, in a lace cap and black dress, but Poll couldn't tell if the picture was taken after the butcher had chopped off her finger because her hand was hidden in the folds of her skirt. There was one of her very much younger, with a baby Aunt Sarah sitting square and solemn eyed on her lap and a tall man behind her, standing to attention like a soldier with his hand on her shoulder. "Is that Grandpa Greengrass?" Poll asked. "No one ever says what happened to him!"

She hoped for a story, but her mother, who was short-tempered that day because a customer was due for a fitting and her dress wasn't ready, just said, "Don't you mention that old rascal to me! He came to a bad end, that's all you need to know!"

In the afternoons, when Theo and Lily and George came home from school, they took turns sitting on the other side of the carbolic sheet and read to her. It was very odd, she thought one day. Her sister and her brothers had become voices to her, reading "Christie's Old Organ," or "Robbery under Arms." She said to Theo, "D'you know, I've forgotten what you look like!"

He was quiet for a minute. Then said, "You'll get a surprise when you see me. I'm growing, like our peppermint pig. Not a peppermint boy any longer."

"Oh, I do wish I could see Johnnie," Poll said.

She heard him that afternoon. He made such a noise in the back garden, squealing and trumpeting, that the sound carried through to Poll's little room in the front of the house. She sat up in bed, rigid and trembling. Something awful was happening—or going to happen! A dreadful thought pierced her mind and invaded her body; her heart and her stomach seemed to come loose inside her and lurch with foreboding. Annie had said, *Our pig didn't half holler!* She pushed shaky legs out of bed and tottered, head swimming, past the carbolic curtain, through her mother's room to the back bedroom. Johnnie's wild protests continued, a shrill hooting and honking that sounded more like ten pigs than one as she struggled with the sash window. Then the noise stopped abruptly. Poll lay across the sill, faint with effort, the summer air cold on her forehead. She moaned, "Johnnie. Oh, Johnnie . . ."

Below, in the garden, her mother was standing at the fence talking to the woman next door. They looked up at Poll in a sudden, shocked silence that seemed, to her terrified mind, a guilty conspiracy.

She said, "Mother . . ."

"What are you doing? You've no business up, you know that! Back to bed with you!"

She seemed to have no breath left. She whispered, "Where's Johnnie?"

"Shut up in the hen house. DO AS YOU'RE TOLD."

She crept back to bed and lay shaking all over, afraid, now she knew Johnnie was safe, of her mother's anger. Suppose she told the doctor and he said, "Off to hospital!"

But when Mother came up, she was smiling. "That dratted pig! D'you know what he's done? Pushed his way through the fence and ate next door's gooseberries. Picked them straight off the bushes, dainty as anything! The whole crop! *She* caught him at it and went after him with a spade and he led her a fine old dance, catch-as-catch-can round the garden! Trouble was, I couldn't stop laughing and that didn't sweeten her temper—once I'd got him shut up, she went for me hammer and tongs, though it's *her* fault he got through her fence, as I told her, and time it was mended! I said I was sorry, of course, all the same, but I couldn't admit liability!" She drew herself up as she said this, back very straight, head lifted proudly. "Then you looked out of the window and that softened her up. Your having been ill, you know. She said she'd forgive him this time, being as he was a special kind of a pig, and gave me an apple for him."

Poll was weak with relief. "Oh, Mother, I thought . . ." Tears choked her voice.

Mother muttered something under her breath, sat down on the bed, and held her hand while she had her cry out. Then she said, "He won't stay shut up in the hen house too long, so you needn't fret about that. I'll get George to mend the old fence soon as he's home. He might not do it for me but he'll do it for Johnnie! You're not the only one softhearted about the old pig, you know!"

"I expect when I get up I'll find he's forgotten me," Poll said mournfully.

But he hadn't. The first day she came down, he trotted into the front room where she lay on the old leather sofa, put his soft twitching nose against the palm of her hand for a moment, then grunted twice and laid his heavy head in her lap.

She said, "Oh, he's *huge*. He's quite different!"

His eyes hadn't changed though. When she pushed back his ears, they seemed to smile up at her: dark blue eyes with long, stiff, lint-pale lashes.

"Too big for the house, really," Mother said.

"Let him stay. Please. He's been lonely for me, you can see! He won't get in your way while you're sewing."

"Just a while then. Long as no one's due for a fitting. Some of my ladies are a bit fussy!"

"I should think they'd be glad to see Johnnie," Poll said, and the pig grunted as if in agreement, then settled comfortably down by the sofa.

Poll talked to him and scratched his back, dividing her attention between him and the privet hawk moth Theo had brought home for her while she was still in bed.

She had had plenty of caterpillars before, kept in an old shoe box with holes in the lid, but she had never cared for them much; their quick, looping walk and the way they waved backward and forward when she blew on them reminded her of Mrs. Marigold Bugg. The privet hawk moth caterpillar was different, more like a little locomotive, smooth skinned and fat and slow moving with a beautiful mauve stripe down his back. Then, later on, he turned into a shining brown chrysalis, and she liked to take him in her hand and watch the warmth make him kick up his tail.

One morning, when she had been downstairs a week, she opened the box and found the chrysalis gone, and there in its place, a moth with gray and pink wings. Poll called, "Oh, Mother, come quickly," and Mother came running, drying her hands on her apron and looking alarmed. "I'm all right," Poll said. "Look!"

She edged the moth onto her finger. He seemed asleep, but when Mother opened the window and Poll held him out in the sunshine, he opened and closed his wings once or twice and then spread them wide, nearly four inches across, and floated away on a soft little wind. They watched him drift up, high over the square. "Time you were out in the air, too," Mother said.

Her head spun at first. She managed to walk, on Mother's arm, as far as Miss Mantripp's cottage and then had to sit down on a chair the old lady put out in the sun for her. The thrush, Kruger, cocked his head and looked down, bright eyed. "You must get him some snails," Miss Mantripp said. "He's very partial to snails."

"I will when I'm strong enough," Poll said. "I don't think I could bend over to look for them just at the moment."

But she was strong enough the next day. She collected snails from Aunt Sarah's rock garden and gave them to Kruger and watched him dash them against the floor of his cage and break them open and eat them. When he had finished, he swelled his plump throat and sang. "He's saying thank you," Miss Mantripp said, and brought her a glass of skim milk. She sat outside Miss Mantripp's front door, drinking the milk, and everyone who passed, even people who were strangers to her, stopped and smiled and said they were glad she was better.

The whole town, it seemed, had been worried about her. When she went shopping with Mother, they were met everywhere by kind, beaming faces, and when they went into Mullen's General Store, old Mullen himself came out of his office and said, "Glad to see you out and about, young woman. There was a time your poor mother thought she might lose you."

That made Poll feel very important. She wouldn't have wanted to die, or to be ill for the rest of her life, but she was a bit sorry that her legs seemed to be fattening up quite so fast and was almost jealous of Theo— although he had grown while she'd been in bed and was now at least an inch taller than she was, he was still very much thinner. When she looked in the mirror she sucked in her cheeks and practiced a faint, hollow smile that made her look sad and interesting.

The day she met Lady March, she had got this smile to perfection. She and Mother were crossing the square on their way to the baker's when a carriage stopped beside them and a high, cracked old voice said, "Oh, Mrs. Greengrass, I am so delighted to see your dear little girl is quite well again!"

Lady March's face was like a piece of thin, crumpled paper under the spread sails of her hat; her fluttering, gloved hands were frail as bird's wings. Poll looked modestly down, smiling her sad, rehearsed smile, and Lady March said, "Poor, pretty child. I'm afraid she still looks very delicate."

"Only when she pulls that silly face," Mother said, rather grimly. She ignored Poll's reproachful sigh and went on, "I'm glad we've met, Lady March. Perhaps you would be kind enough to tell your daughter her new dress is ready whenever she wishes to call and collect it."

This dress, as Poll knew, had been ready for more than two weeks and the most likely reason why Arabella March had not come to fetch it was that she had overspent her quarter's allowance. Only that morning Mother had looked in her purse and said, with an angry sniff, "I suppose not paying what they owe is one of the ways rich people save money."

Lady March laughed with a sound like glass tinkling. "I expect she forgot, my dear, you know what girls are! But I'll remind her, of course. I know she's been really quite pleased with the work you have done for her up to now. As a matter of fact, I might ask you to do something for me! Not a *new* gown—as you know, I always get my things made at Mullen's. So much more convenient to be able to get the material there and put it down on the bill, don't you know? But I have an afternoon gown that needs renovating and I have never found Mrs. Bugg very helpful with alterations. Won't take the trouble, I suppose; it's the same story wherever you turn nowadays, standards of service are not what they used to be! But then I expect you know that as well as I do!"

"Oh, yes," Mother said. "Yes, Lady March."

"I'll bring you the gown, then?" She smiled graciously, as if the gown was a present. "Would this afternoon be convenient?"

"I'm afraid not, Lady March. Not this week at all. One of my customers has a funeral on Friday and that, as you know, really must take priority!"

The manservant driving the carriage had been sitting still on the box and staring straight ahead all this time. He cleared his throat suddenly and Mother's mouth twitched. A purplish color crept into Lady March's cheeks as if she felt she was being laughed at in some way. Poll felt sorry for her and looked at Mother indignantly but Mother's expression was innocent.

Lady March said, "Well, next week, perhaps? To tell you the truth, Mrs. Greengrass, one reason I am anxious to come is to see your famous pet pig. The one everyone is talking about. When I spoke to the Vicar last Sunday, he mentioned it and said it really was a remarkable animal. I know, Mrs. Greengrass! I have a *splendid* idea! Would you be kind enough to bring him up to the Manor one day? Round to the back door and show me his tricks?" She clapped her little hands together in affected excitement and added, "Of course, you could pick up the gown at the same time, couldn't you?"

Mother gave her a long, hard, pitying look and shook her head slowly. "My Johnnie is not a back door or kitchen pig, Lady March! Nor does he do *tricks,* like a freak in a fair! As the Vicar has told you, he is an unusual creature and he has his own proper dignity that I wouldn't wish to offend. A formal invitation to visit you would be a different matter, of course."

The manservant took a red handkerchief out of his pocket and blew his nose loudly. The noise startled the horse and the carriage jerked forward over the cobbles. The man looked over his shoulder and grinned.

Mother smiled pleasantly. "Good morning, Lady March. You will give my message to your daughter, won't you?" She took Poll's hand and walked on. Once out of earshot, she chuckled. "Really, the cheek of the woman!"

Poll said, puzzled, "She only wanted to see Johnnie."

"Just a sprat to catch a mackerel, Poll. Mullen's won't do alterations at a price she's willing to pay, that's the truth of it. Well, I won't either! I may have sunk down in the world but not so low that I'm ready to turn seams on an old miser's gown for a shilling and a kind word or two! That's the last we'll hear of that, I do hope!"

She was wrong. The next day the manservant came to the door with a note on an engraved card.

> *Lady March would be pleased if*
> *Mrs. Greengrass, her younger*
> *daughter, and her pet pig would*
> *care to take tea with her next*
> *Friday at four.*

Mother sat in the kitchen and laughed. "She's beaten me," she gasped. "Oh, she's a sly one! Run to the door, Poll, and tell the man we'll be delighted to come. No—wait a minute, I'll write, since we're being so grand with each other!"

Poll watched her write. She said, "Shall you alter her dress after all?"

Mother put her note in an envelope and stuck the flap down. "Oh, yes, she's earned it. Outsmarted me properly, and it's always best to pay up with a good grace when that happens. If she's willing to entertain an old pig in her drawing room just to get a bit of work done on the cheap, then good luck to her!"

Mother scrubbed Johnnie down with the broom— since he liked having his back scratched he found this no hardship—and left him to dry in the sun while she and Poll dressed. Poll wore her pink shantung with a hanging pocket to match and her leghorn hat trimmed with daisies. "Now you're fit to have tea with a queen," Mother said.

They set off at twenty minutes to four, Johnnie walking sedately behind them, across the Market Square, past the church, and took a shortcut through the ruins of the old priory on the edge of the town. When they started up the long drive that led to the Manor House, Poll began to feel nervous. She looked at her mother and saw her lips moving silently, as if she were holding an internal conversation. Then Mother made a little grimace and smiled. Her eyes shone suddenly bright and, when she spoke, her voice was light and eager as bird song. She said, "Polly, love, forget the unkind things I said about Lady March. She's not a bad old thing, really," and Poll thought at first she was just saying this because she felt happy and wanted everything to be pleasant about her. But then she added, "It's hard to be lonely and old and know that even your servants laugh at you when your back's turned," and Poll remembered the man snorting into his handkerchief and grinning on the box of the carriage and knew it was true.

He had the same knowing grin on his face when he opened the door to them, and it made Poll indignant. Copying her mother, she averted her gaze and ignored his impertinence. It was harder to ignore the two young maids giggling at the far end of the hall, particularly when she knew they were not just laughing at the sight of a pig walking in the front entrance and at foolish old Lady March for inviting him, but at her and her mother too for joining in this daft game. She did her best. She gave them one look and put her nose in the air and followed Mother and Johnnie into the drawing room, where a log fire was burning in spite of the warmth of the day.

Johnnie went straight to it as if he was accustomed to being received like a gentleman. Lady March, looking small and witchlike without her big hat, scratched his ears tentatively and he sat down by her chair and leaned against her. "Oh," she said. "Oh, my!"

"Push him away if he's heavy," Mother said. "He won't hurt you. Or your carpets either. He's as well trained as a good dog in that way."

"I've never had a dog in my drawing room either," Lady March said.

One of the maids brought in tea. She was still giggling openly and, when Lady March motioned her to put the tray down on a low table beside her, she dumped it down with a rough air of contempt that Poll recognized as deliberate—she wanted the visitors to know how little she thought of her mistress! Lady March laughed as if she were not embarrassed at all, only amused at the girl's clumsiness, but when the maid had gone she looked at the tray and said, "Oh, dear,

Cook has forgotten the sugar," in a tone that said, clearly as if she had spoken the words, "I'm afraid if I ring the bell, she'll be rude again."

Mother said, "Poll and I don't have sugar in tea, Lady March, but if you want it, Poll can run to the kitchen."

Lady March said she didn't take sugar either. She poured tea and offered them bread and butter and cake. The bread and butter had been cut a long time and was curling at the edges and the jam had a film of dust over it as if the dish had been left standing uncovered by the side of a fire, but the cake was all right, a rich, dark fruitcake that no one could spoil. Poll ate three slices and answered Lady March's questions. Yes, she was very much better. No, she wasn't back at school yet, but she would be next week. Yes, she was looking forward to it—she heard herself saying this with surprise and wondered if she could really mean it.

When the conversation about school was finished, Lady March talked to Mother about patterns and materials and the latest Paris fashions. Poll sat in a big chair, pins and needles in her dangling feet, and tried not to yawn. At last tea was over, and when Lady March took Mother upstairs to look at the gown that had to be altered, Poll escaped into the garden with Johnnie. She went round the side of the house into the stable yard and peeped through the window into the kitchen. The man who doubled as coachman and butler was sitting with his feet on the table, the two young maids sat either side of him, and a fat woman in a black dress and apron presided over the teapot. There was a splendid spread on the table: muffins, a crusty new loaf, cheese, butter, jam, and several sorts of cake. Poll thought of Lady March's tea tray laid out with stale bread and dusty jam and felt herself swelling with anger in a way she had not done for ages. The last time was before she ran off to see Annie Dowsett, before she was ill.

The other side of the yard there was a rose garden and beyond that, a small wood, full of foxgloves. Full of maybugs, too; the air whirred with them. Poll knocked one down with her hat and picked it up as it lay stunned on the ground. Its little horny feet tickled her palm. She put it into her handkerchief pocket and went on knocking down the flying beetles until she had a buzzing, angry pocketful. She felt the weight of the pocket in her hand and thought of Lily, who was scared of maybugs, who went wild if one came into the bedroom at night because she was afraid it would get into her hair.

She went back to the stable yard and looked in the kitchen window again. They were still sitting there, stuffing themselves. One of the girls said something and they all roared with laughter, wet, greedy mouths open. The man belched loudly and slapped his stomach.

The window was open at the bottom. Poll loosed the thread of her handkerchief pocket and emptied the maybugs over the sill with a jerk of her wrist. Fright, or rage, at being shut up made them buzz louder than ever now they were free, and within seconds the girls and the fat cook were on their feet screaming, beating frantic hands in the air, running round the room, banging into each other, knocking chairs over. The man jumped up too. He saw Poll at the window and she put her thumbs in her ears and waggled her fingers and stuck out her tongue at him before she ran off.

Johnnie was sitting patiently on the path in front of the house. Poll reached him as her mother and Lady March came out of the door. Mother was saying, "I'll speak to Mrs. Dowsett, then, and bring Annie to see you . . ."

But Lady March was looking at Poll. She said, in a surprised voice, "Why, the child looks quite different. Much better than she did earlier on, don't you know?"

Mother smiled. "You wouldn't think she'd ever been ill to look at her."

"Oh, I'm better," Poll said. "I started to be better about two minutes ago and I'm quite better now."

7

Theo said, "If Mother grumbles about someone to start with, you can be sure she'll end up taking their part. I bet you anything Lady March will be someone she has to take care of, like Annie Dowsett."

Annie was often in their house now. She was shy with George and Lily and Theo but she worshipped Mother, following round at her heels "just like the old pig," Lily said—though she was careful not to let Mother hear this. "Annie's a good girl," Mother said. "She just needs encouragement."

When Annie left school at Christmas she was going into service with Lady March at the Manor House. "That's a good turn done for them both," Mother said when she arranged this. "The poor old soul needs someone who doesn't look down on her. I told her, if I were you I'd get rid of those flibbertigibbet girls and get someone respectful. And it'll be a fine place for Annie. My mother went to the Manor House as kitchen maid and ended up cook, no reason why Annie shouldn't do just as well. She's got a nice light hand with pastry already."

"I can cook too," Poll said. "I can make lovely buns, better than Annie's. I wish I could leave school and go and be a cook too."

"Don't let your Aunt Sarah hear you say that," Mother said. "She'd think it a disgrace for her niece to go into service. She'd never hold her head up again!"

"Granny Greengrass was a cook. And your mother. Why can't I be?"

"You're luckier. You've got a chance to rise up."

"I think Annie's lucky," Poll said enviously. "I wish I could leave school. School's boring. I hate it."

She was only there mornings because she was still thought to be delicate, and although she was quite glad to be back at first, for a change, that wore off quite soon. Her classroom looked over Farmer Tuft's meadow. The window was open at the bottom in fine weather and Poll, dreaming at her desk throughout the math lessons, could hear Farmer Tuft's cows plucking the squeaky grass, and the frogs in the pond splashing and croaking. A willow tree hung over the pond and she could see a magpie in its top branches. *One for sorrow,* Poll thought, watching its long tail flick up and down, but her only sorrow at the moment was vulgar fractions.

"I'm afraid Poll will never be a worker like Lily and George and she isn't naturally clever like Theo," Aunt Sarah said. "I really don't know what we'll do with her!"

"Plenty of time," Aunt Harriet said. "Leave her be, she'll make something of herself yet."

"If you've got nothing better to do, Poll," Mother said, "you can find a bit of emery paper and clean that steel fender."

Poll found something better to do. In the afternoons, while everyone else was locked up in school, she kept out of Mother's way and roamed, free as air. She went to Bride's Pit and, if there were no Gypsies there, poked the water buttercups away with a stick and picked up the horrid black leeches that crawled on the sandy bottom near the edge of the water. Or she explored the woods, kicking puffballs into dust clouds and keeping a sharp lookout for Keeper Green. Sometimes, if it was hot and she was feeling lazy, she just crossed the square and went down Tank Lane and climbed an old elm tree and watched the world go by.

Not that many people came down Tank Lane. Tramps sometimes; Mr. Snoop, the postman, with the two cows he grazed on the lush roadside verges; the rabbit skin man, a long stick with rabbits skewered on it over his shoulder; Percy, the washerwoman's son, who helped his mother by fetching and carrying the washing in a wooden box on wheels. Percy was dumb except for a queer noise he made in his throat, midway between a croup and a crow—hoo*up,* hoo*up*—as he pushed his old box along, dipping his head up and down like a bird drinking. He passed up and down Tank Lane several times most afternoons while Poll kept watch in the elm tree, and the squeal of his cart wheels and his croupy singsong were part of the dreaming summer days, like the feel and the pungent smell of the hairy elm leaves when she squeezed them between her hot fingers.

She saw Lily once, wheeling her bicycle with the handsome, wooden-legged Vicar limping beside her, and giggled privately when Mother said later on, after supper, "What are you so cock-a-hoop about, Lily? You look like a cat that's been at the cream."

Another day, she saw Theo and Noah Bugg. They were walking along like friends, heads together, and she noticed, surprised, that Theo was almost as tall as Noah now. She heard Noah laugh and say, "You'll have to think of something else then, won't you, if you want to keep on." Theo said something she couldn't catch and Noah laughed again. "Give over then, Greengrass. 'S'all one to me!" He walked off, whistling, and Theo stood and stared after him. When Poll called out softly, he looked up and turned red as a poppy.

"You spying on me?" he said, as she slid down the tree.

"What are you blushing about?"

"I'm not."

"Yes, you are. I can see your face, can't I?"

"You scared me, that's all."

"No, it isn't." She saw his sly, silly smile, his eyes

puckering up at the corners. "He's still teasing you, is he?"

"Blackmailing's the word!"

"Because of that *egg* you stole? But that's *stupid!*"

"You didn't think so at the time," he reminded her. "You were scared he'd tell Aunt Sarah and that she'd be so disgusted she'd cast us all off. Hell Fire for Thieves and Liars. The Workhouse, anyway!"

He was laughing at her. She said, "That's not fair," and gave an indignant sniff, like her mother. "I was only young then. I didn't know any better. It's not fair blaming me!"

He kicked a loose stone on the road. "I'm not, really. You were right in a way. Not about the work-house, of course, or him telling Aunt Sarah—he'd be too scared for that—but he might have told Mrs. Bugg, and it would have upset Mother if she'd spread the tale round. Like Mrs. Bugg said, *blood will out.* I mean, there was that trouble when Dad left his firm and I thought, suppose Mrs. Bugg knows and wants to make something of it? It 'ud give her a fine chance if she knew I'd been caught stealing too! Well, not *too,* because Dad didn't take any money, but you know what I mean."

"No, I don't," Poll burst out. "You're just mud-dling me up like you always do. Muddling yourself as well, I should think."

"You un-muddle me, then!"

He looked so wretched that she felt sorry. Poor Theo! He was older than she was, and cleverer, but sometimes it seemed that being clever just made him unhappy. She said, "Well, it was such a long time ago, wasn't it? Ages and ages. If Noah went sneaking now, no one would listen."

He shook his head. "It's not as simple as that, I'm afraid. Trouble is, once you start a thing, you get caught up and it all gets more complicated." He squatted on his haunches and picked up several small flints, then threw them up and caught them on the back of his hand. When he had done this four times, he dribbled the flints through his fingers and said in a sad, hollow voice, "Aunt Sarah would say, 'What a tangled web we weave when once we practice to deceive.' "

"What's that got to do with it?"

He looked at her, then stood up and sighed. "I've said things to Noah that I shouldn't and that I wouldn't like to get out. Just to keep him quiet in the beginning, and then as a sort of game."

"A game?" She was quite bewildered now.

"A story, then."

"What about?"

"If I told you, you'd hate me. I hate *myself*."

"Because of a *story?* Stories can't hurt anyone."

"Lies can though. If you tell *lies* . . ." He looked at her desperately. "Please, Poll, don't ask me to tell you. I'd rather *die*. Really!"

"You're always saying that!" She thought for a moment. "Was it lies about *me?*"

"No."

"Will you tell me sometime?"

He screwed his eyes up. "I might. Yes, I expect so."

"That's not good enough!"

"I'll tell you before—before your next birthday."

"Promise?"

"I promise."

He spat on his finger, dried it on his jacket, then drew it across his throat, making a gurgling sound.

Poll smiled. "All right." He blinked at her and she added generously, "And I promise not to ask before then!"

She would be ten in September. It was only July now and, as they walked home, it began to seem a long time to wait. She wished she had insisted he must tell her earlier, next week perhaps, but she had promised now. And his serious look made her feel serious too, old and responsible, so that when he said, "I've got a penny, Poll, what would you like? Sherbet suckers or Cupid's Whispers? We've time to go to the shop before tea," she was hurt. Did he think she was a baby to be bribed with sweets?

She said haughtily, "I don't want anything, thank you, you can keep your rotten old penny *and* your rotten old secret. I don't suppose it's even worth knowing," and ran on ahead, tight-lipped and angry.

Although she continued to feel deeply injured and let Theo know it, pretending she hadn't heard whenever he spoke to her and being extra nice to Lily and George in his presence to make the point sharper, she couldn't keep it up. Theo was so quiet, so meek and withdrawn, that there was no fun in tormenting him. And besides, so much was happening just at this moment, the summer suddenly exploding like a firework into a sparkling burst of excitement, she had no time left to brood.

The end of term first; a week later, the Sunday School Treat to the sea in two hay wagons drawn by spruced-up shire horses, coats gleaming like satin; and then, at the beginning of August, the King's Coronation.

That was a perfect day from beginning to end. Trestle tables were set up in the square, the whole town had a huge meal of roast beef and plum pudding, and afterward there were races and games in the big Vicarage garden. Poll and Annie were among the girls chosen to dance round the maypole, wearing white dresses with fluttering ribbons, and Lily played the harmonium, brought out of the Church Hall for the occasion. There were races for everyone: egg-and-spoon and three-legged for the children and a comic obstacle course for grownups that Aunt Harriet won, losing her hat as she wriggled through an open-ended beer barrel and beating Mrs. Snoop, the postman's wife, in a close finish. George had too much beer with his beef and had to lie down most of the afternoon, but he recovered in time for the fancy dress ball in the Assembly Rooms in the evening. The chandeliers tinkled and the floor shook with thumping feet; everyone danced, even Aunt Sarah, who did a dignified waltz with the headmaster of the boys' school, and Lily's copper curls flew as she whirled round in the arms of one young man after another. Poll, watching her, thought she had never seen anyone look so happy and beautiful. She was so happy herself it made her heart sore, a bruised ball of joy in her chest, and when she won first prize for the Little Boy Blue costume Mother had made her and everyone clapped and stamped with delight, it was all she could do not to cry.

One moment it seemed that the lovely evening would go on forever; the next, they were out in the still, starry night, going home. Poll clutched her prize, a big box of chocolates tied with striped ribbon, and Mother carried the hunting horn Aunt Sarah had lent Poll to go with her costume—a real hunting horn that had belonged to a long-dead great-uncle. Aunt Harriet picked up her skirts and skipped like a girl, and Lily danced backward in front of them all and said breathlessly, "Did you hear what the Vicar said to old Mr. Pocock this afternoon? He said, 'That girl's got nice legs,' and he meant me. I heard him!"

Aunt Sarah said, "I thought that dress was too short! You must lengthen it before she wears it again, Emily."

Mother nodded meekly, but her eyes shone. She put the hunting horn to her lips and, standing in the middle of the wide Market Square, blew a long wailing blast that echoed back from the houses and silenced

141

them all. Poll looked at her family as the beautiful, sad, haunted sound died away and felt weak with happiness because she loved them so much. She saw Theo smiling at her as if he knew how she felt; she smiled back and forgave him forever.

She said, "This is the best day of my life," and they all smiled at her.

Aunt Harriet said, "Bless you, Poll, this is nothing. You just wait till you've seen a good Harvest Fair!"

George went harvesting and Poll and Theo carried his dinner out in a basket and sometimes stayed to watch till the field was finished. As the cutter clattered round, the square of wheat in the middle grew smaller and smaller until the terrified rabbits sheltering there came shooting out, ears laid back, zigzagging wildly over the stubble while everyone shouted and chased them with sticks. Theo once caught a small rabbit but Poll never did, and finally the farmer gave her a dead one to take home to her mother. There was dust on its eyes and dark blood at the side of its mouth and it stretched out across her arms, stiff and straight as if it was running still. Poll saw the farmer's wife watching her and said, "Poor rabbit," in a sad voice and stroked its long ears, and the farmer's wife smiled.

They had rabbit stew for supper that night, fragrant with herbs from the garden, and Theo said, "Smells almost as good as a Gypsy stew. D'you know how Gypsies cook hedgehogs? They roll them in clay and bake them in ashes and the skin comes off with the clay, prickles and all, clean as a whistle."

The Gypsies came into town several days before the Harvest Fair and camped in the Priory ruins. They kept themselves apart from the other Fair people and spoke their own language. Poll and Theo lingered round their caravans just to hear the flood of strange, bubbling words, although the Gypsies often fell silent if they came too close, and stared at them with dark, gleaming eyes. But they were friendly enough when they came to the door, selling wooden pegs and cotton lace and birds for the pot that they always called "pigeons." "Pigeons, my foot!" Mother said, when one of them offered her a cock pheasant, but the man laughed and said it was a Japanese peacock.

After the Gypsies, the rest of the Fair began to arrive and the Market Square filled up with great wagons and caravans carrying tents and sideshows and merry-go-rounds. Some of the caravans were painted with pictures to show what was inside: sword-swallowers and fat ladies and two-headed calves. The picture of the Fire Eater was the best, a giant dressed in red satin knee breeches and lace-ruffled shirt, spouting yellow flame from his mouth, but when Poll and Theo hung round, hoping to see him, the only person who got down from the caravan was a short, bald man with a squint.

The day of the Fair, Poll woke up early and went mushrooming. The best mushrooms grew in a field that belonged to a notoriously bad-tempered farmer, but Poll was lucky this morning: she had a full basket by the time he appeared in the gateway, yelling and waving his stick. "Tan your backside for you if I catch you again," he roared after her as she wriggled through the gap in the hedge, and when her heart had stopped pounding, she sang as she ran down the lane to show she wasn't scared by that rude, silly threat—Aunt Harriet had said he wouldn't dare lay a finger on respectable citizens.

The back door was open and Johnnie was sitting on the step in the sun. She gave him a handful of blackberries she had picked on the way home and put the basket of mushrooms inside the kitchen. Then, hearing her mother's step on the stairs, she darted into the garden before she could be asked to lay the table for breakfast.

Out of sight, out of mind—that was the best course when you might be asked to do something! Safer in Aunt Sarah's garden, she thought, and went through the wooden gate, Johnnie behind her. "You keep to the path," she warned him. "Aunt Sarah won't like it if you trample her flower beds." And he walked at her heels, dignified as a mayor or an alderman.

Halfway up the cinder path she saw a twist of smoke rising from the summerhouse and stopped dead. Aunt Sarah sometimes lit a fire there in winter, but rarely in summer, and never at this time of the morning! She waited a minute, feeling uncertain, and then marched up and pushed the door open.

An old man was sitting by the fire, roasting an onion stuck on the end of a knife. Poll said sternly,

"Don't you know this place is private? What are you doing here?"

He turned his head slowly. He had a stubbly gray beard and long hair so thin that his pink scalp showed through.

He said, "I might ask you that. Who are you?" and Poll was so surprised that he didn't speak in broad Norfolk that she answered at once, and politely.

"I'm Poll. Poll Greengrass. This summerhouse belongs to my aunt."

"Oh," he said. "Is that who you are?" and looked her up and down with an amused smile that made her feel oddly uncomfortable. He was looking her over as if he wasn't a tramp, stealing a night's lodging, but someone who had as much right here as she had. He yawned hugely, scratched his beard with the hand that wasn't holding the knife and the onion, and said, "Since you're here, you can run an errand for me. Go and tell those great, idle girls I'd like a good piece of fat belly pork for my breakfast."

"D'you mean *Aunt Sarah?*"

"Harriet will do just as well. Get along with you. Tell 'em I'm hungry."

She backed away slowly, then ran down the path. She put Johnnie through the gate into his own garden and went to Aunt Sarah's kitchen. Both aunts were there. She said, uncertainly, "There's a man in the summerhouse. He says he wants breakfast."

To her amazement, they took this quite calmly.

Aunt Sarah smiled and Aunt Harriet said, "Oh, he's turned up again, has he? I thought it was about time. Last time anyone saw him, it was your father, in London."

Aunt Sarah said, "I believe James set him up for the winter. He's always been good in that way."

They both spoke as if it were perfectly natural for an old tramp to spend the night in their summerhouse and then order his breakfast!

Aunt Sarah rose from the table and went to the larder and Aunt Harriet said to Poll, "Go and tell your mother. She might have some things of your father's he won't need anymore. Tell her a pair of boots would be useful, they take the same size."

"Boots for the *tramp?*"

Her aunts looked at each other. Then Aunt Sarah sighed. "I suppose that's what he must look like! Poor Father! He's your grandfather, Poll. Grandpa Greengrass."

Poll stared. Aunt Harriet said, "What's that open mouth for? Catching flies, or a bus?" Poll closed her mouth and her aunt went on briskly, "Since you don't seem to know, I'd best tell you. Some people are foot-loose and your grandfather's one. He wanted to be an actor when he was a young man, but *his* father said there was no money in that and apprenticed him to a stonemason. But a settled life didn't suit him, and he took to the road. He's happy that way and he doesn't bother us often. That good enough for you?"

Poll swallowed saliva and nodded. Several things that had not made sense before had fallen into place in her mind. Hidden under the table, sent there for naughtiness, she had heard her parents talking about Grandpa Greengrass. He had turned up at Rowland and Son the day the money was stolen and Father had been afraid they would send the police after him because he looked like a tramp so Father took the blame himself. By the time he was sure Young Rowland had been the thief, the idea of going off to America had taken root in his mind. Theo had said he wanted adventure but Mother had blamed Grandpa Greengrass. She had said, "I knew he'd bring us all down one day," and when Poll had seen his picture in the photograph album Mother had called him an "old rascal."

If she really felt that, she wouldn't want to give him Father's old clothes! More likely, she'd fly into one of her tempers and say, "I'll see him in hell first."

But, in fact, she just sniffed when Poll told her and said, "Yes, of course, poor old fellow," and went straight upstairs. Poll waited in the kitchen, listening to drawers being opened and closed overhead, and then Theo came down, a bundle in his arms and a queer grin on his face.

She said, "What's that silly grin for?" and he put his finger to his lips, warning her.

He was still grinning as he followed her into the garden. As soon as he was sure no one could hear them, he said, "That's one thing got rid of! Those ghastly pink vests. I got them out of the camphor chest while Mother had her back turned."

Poll giggled. "They'll be too small for him."

"They've stretched. They'll fit anyone. I hoped I'd grow out of them but they grew *with* me, and when Mother put them away for the summer she said they were good as new. I was scared I'd have to wear them the rest of my life!"

"Won't Aunt Sarah be cross?"

"She hardly can, can she? I'll tell her I thought my grandfather's need was greater than mine." He stopped grinning. "What's he like, Poll? Does he look like anyone in our family?"

"I don't know. I mean, I didn't know who he was so I wouldn't think, would I?" She looked at Theo. Something seemed familiar but she couldn't think what it was. Then she knew. "He's got eyes just like yours," she said.

They put the bundle down inside the summerhouse. He was sitting at Aunt Sarah's desk, tucking into bread and bacon and tea. He had loosened his shirt in the front and, although his face and neck were dirty, the skin of his chest was white and smooth.

When Poll said, "We've brought you some clothes," he nodded, but paid no more attention until he had finished his meal.

Then he sat back, chasing bacon scraps caught in

his teeth with his tongue, and said, "Two others, aren't there? An older boy and a girl?"

"Lily and George," Theo said. He blinked and added, "Sir," in a doubtful voice, as if he wasn't sure how to address this interesting but unlikely relation.

Poll felt strange, too. This tramp was her grandfather! No one else she knew had a tramp in their family! It was different—and rather exciting. She wondered how old he was. Mother had only been twelve when Grandma Greengrass had died! She couldn't ask him because it was rude to ask grown-ups how old they were. But she ought to say *something!*

She said, "We're going to have mushrooms for breakfast. I picked them this morning."

His eyes rested on her without very much interest. Blue eyes, like Theo's.

She tried again. "I know a good mushroom field. The farmer chases you out, but it's the best place, and you have to be careful with mushrooms. I once found one in a wood, a huge one, big as a dinner plate, but it turned yellow in the pan and Mother threw it away."

He tipped his chair back and looked at the ceiling and yawned.

Theo whispered, "Come away, Poll. He doesn't want to talk to us."

Poll could see that. Her grandfather wasn't in the least interested in her or in Theo—or in anyone in their family. He couldn't ever have been, because he had left

149

them. To go off and leave Grandma Greengrass was one thing because she was only his wife, no real blood relation, but he had gone off and left his own children—Aunt Sarah and Aunt Harriet and Uncle Edmund and Father—who were!

But he was *her* relation, too. Her grandfather! And even if that didn't matter to him, it mattered to her! She had never seen him before and might never see him again. Never, in her whole life! She wanted to do something to mark the occasion but she couldn't think what. If only she had something to give him, a present of some kind, or some money to spend. Father had given him money last winter but another winter was coming and Father was in America. And she had no money. She had spent last Saturday's penny and, although Aunt Sarah and Mother had promised to give them all something to spend at the Fair, they hadn't done so yet. That was a good thing in a way, because if she had it already she would have felt bound to give it to him and it would have been dreadful to be without money to spend at the Fair!

Then she thought of something. Such a marvelous idea that she laughed aloud. She ran out of the summerhouse, round the back, and sank onto her knees. The earth was loose as if someone had been digging there recently but she didn't understand why until she had the tin in her hand and took the lid off. There was nothing inside except a few grains of dust.

"It's gone," she said. "The gold's gone!"

"Yes," Theo said. He was standing behind her. She turned and looked up and saw his shamed, nervous grin. He said, "I was going to tell you . . ."

8

"You gave it to Noah?" Poll said. And then, because Theo was staring at her so blankly, like a foreigner or a deaf person, repeated it louder. "You gave all that *gold* to Noah Bugg?"

"It wasn't worth anything," Theo said.

They were sitting on the log pile in the small arbor at the end of Aunt Sarah's garden, a good private place, covered with willow and with its back to the summerhouse.

"Of course gold's worth something," Poll said. "Even a small piece. A gold sovereign's worth something, isn't it?"

Theo said patiently, "Not gold leaf shavings though. Why d'you think Dad brought them home for us to make Christmas cards with? Just what was left over, that's all they were. Sweepings off the floor."

She gasped. "But you *said* . . ."

"I know what I said. I thought . . ." He screwed up his face, trying to remember exactly what he had thought, all those months ago. "I really did think, just for a bit, that they must be worth something. Otherwise, why should Dad go off like he did? It didn't make sense. I mean, I didn't know about Grandpa Greengrass then." He looked at her accusingly. "You didn't tell me."

"I didn't know either, did I? Not that it was *him* who'd turned up, because I thought he was dead."

"When you were under the table you heard Dad say *my father*. You said so just now."

No answer to that! Or Poll couldn't think of one. She wailed, "You're not fair," and wished he was still smaller than she was so she could hit him. Then she thought of something better than hitting. She said, "You made up a story, didn't you? You're always making up stories. Things that aren't true. Like—like saying the Swineherd wasn't just a poor man who had a dream and found gold under the oak tree, but a thief who'd buried it there! You buried *our* gold and said *Dad* was a thief!" She was so angry she hissed in and out as if her breath was fire, burning her. "Oh, that was mean!"

He said, "Yes, I know," and sat staring at her. He looked hypnotized, his eyes glassy.

She felt powerful and proud. She thought for a minute, pretending to be watching a spider in the willow branches over her head. When it plummeted down and hung, spinning on its gossamer thread, she said sharply, "Did Noah believe the gold was valuable, then? Did you tell him it was?"

He nodded.

"Did he believe you?"

"Not at first, I don't think . . ." His eyes begged her to let him off but she sat stiffly, cold as a judge, and he went on reluctantly, "So I told him Dad had stolen it from the coach firm in London to make sure we had something to live on while he was away in America. I thought that made it sound more likely, somehow. I don't think he believed me, or not altogether, but it was like a game. Half a game, anyway. And I suppose he didn't want to make trouble so he decided to play it. He said, all right, then, long as I gave him a piece of gold every week he'd keep his mouth shut. About— about *everything!* It was a way of making friends, really. Sharing a secret. Do you understand?" He smiled at her wanly. "If you don't now, you will when you're older."

Poll was outraged. How old did he think she was? *Five?* She said, "You mean you told him lies about Dad stealing gold for a *game?*"

She put her face so close to his that she could see her face in his eyes. He closed them, as if to get rid of

her, and said, "Daft, I see now! I told you it was something awful I'd done. That I'd die rather than tell you.
Well, I'd rather die *now*."

"Don't ask me to pity you," Poll said witheringly.
But she did, all the same. He looked so despairing and
he was such a fool! She said, "I suppose it's being so
clever makes you so stupid. You get tangled up. Look at
the mess you're in now! No more gold to give Noah, so
what'll he do? What if he goes round telling everyone
our father's a thief?"

"That *I said he was*. That's what's important."

"What'll Mother think? And Aunt Sarah?"

Theo shivered and groaned. "I wish I was dead."

"That wouldn't help much. If Noah was, it
might."

"That's wicked, Poll!"

"Why?"

He looked at her astonished face carefully, then
sighed and said, "No, it isn't. I mean, you're not
wicked. Just me."

Poll said, "You could give Noah your Fair
money." She paused. "Mine too, if you like."

He shook his head. "That wouldn't help much.
Not in the end. I've got to do something that'll stop
him forever . . ."

He wrapped his arms round himself and sat huddled up as if he felt suddenly cold. His face grew
pinched and determined.

155

Poll said, "We'd better go and have breakfast. I've been up for hours; I feel *hollow.*"

When they passed the summerhouse, Grandpa Greengrass was fast asleep in the chair, mouth open and snoring. But when Poll crept up and peeped in the window later that morning, he had packed up and gone.

Mother said, "Oh, he wouldn't hang around. He's got some decent feelings."

"I wish I could just clear off when I felt like it," Theo said. "I wish *I* was a tramp."

"Cold in winter," Poll said. "Poor old man."

Mother sniffed. "Don't waste your pity, my girl. If you want to be sorry for someone, give a thought to Aunt Sarah! What a cross to bear all these years! The shame of it, when she has a position to keep up in the town."

"Aunt Sarah wasn't ashamed," Poll said. "She said, *poor Father,* and she gave him breakfast."

"She's a better Christian than I am," Mother said. "She'd give the Devil the shirt off her back if she thought he was chilly. Now get out from under my feet, both of you, and let me get on. Go down to Tuft's farm, Poll, and get a can of skim milk. A milk and leek soup will set us all up for the Fair."

The long day passed. Poll went to Tuft's farm and got the skim milk and on the way home whirled the can round her head without spilling a drop. The water cart was out in the square laying the dust, and she put the can down and ran in and out of the sparkly shower to cool off.

It was so hot. Mother made her lie down in the afternoon in case she got overheated. She never thought she would sleep but she did, and when Aunt Harriet came up to wake her, it was alrady half dark and the Fair music was coming in through her window, a magical, tinny sound on the blue air.

"Makes me feel young again," Aunt Harriet said. Her ruddy face was polished with pleasure. "Buck up, slowcoach! We'll take Theo and go, we won't wait for the others."

"Walk up, walk up, ladies and gentlemen, chance of a lifetime to see the World's Fattest Lady. Satisfaction guaranteed, only sixpence." The booths had raised platforms in front with men shouting their wares. "Roll up, roll up, see the Marvel of Nature, the Elephant Man with a Genuine Trunk." The men were called barkers, Aunt Harriet said, and you couldn't believe all they said—she had seen the Elephant Man the year before last and there was nothing marvelous about him at all, he only had an extra-long nose.

Naphtha flames roared and shivered and flared yellow ribbons of flame on the wind, lighting up gingerbread stalls that sold gingerbread houses spread with white icing; hoopla and coconut shies; the booth where you could have a tooth pulled for sixpence or watch it being done to someone else for a penny; and, best and most beautiful, the big merry-go-round with its sailing horses and peacocks and unicorns and its sweet, grinding tune that played on and on . . .

The moon shines tonight on pretty Redwing,
My pretty Redwing,
The breeze is dying,
The night birds crying . . .

Theo went to see the Fire Eater and Poll paid threepence to see the Tiniest Woman in England. There was a toy house in the tent and the Tiniest Woman peeped out of one of the windows. Poll paid her money and went round the back to shake hands with her. She had been bending down to look out of the window, but she was still much smaller than Poll even when she stood up, a merry midget whose little hand was hard and horny as an old man's. She squeezed Poll's fingers and said, "God bless you, my darling."

They went on the merry-go-round, Theo on a prancing horse with flaring red nostrils and Poll on an ostrich. The seat was slippery and she clutched its neck while she swooped and soared and the music played "Pretty Redwing" and the colored world flew round faster and faster. She saw her mother and shouted, "Look at me, look at me," and drummed her feet on the side of the ostrich, but the next time round, Mother had vanished.

Theo cried out, "Look, Poll, look . . ." craning round so he almost fell off his horse. He was red faced and crowing with laughter. "Look, *Johnnie,*" he screamed, and as the merry-go-round began to slow down, Poll saw their pig galloping past, Mother and George running after him. He was twisting and turning, a great, lumbering, lolloping pig, going mad with excitement as other people shouted and joined in the chase. "How'd he get out?" Theo said, as he dropped from his horse to the still-moving platform, then to the ground.

Poll was slower. By the time she was off the ostrich, she had lost sight of them all. She ran round the merry-go-round, crashed into someone who said, "Watch where you're going," and when she looked up she saw Noah Bugg's pale eyes gleaming down at her. He held her by the shoulders but she kicked his shin to make him let go and ran wildly on, shouting, "Johnnie, oh, Johnnie . . ."

He came charging toward her like a live cannonball, his pursuers behind him. Poll held out her arms to stop him and he swerved, grunting, and shot through the open flap of a tent. There was a horrendous crescendo of squealing and shouting, the canvas sides of the tent shook and bulged, and then a huge woman with a straggling gray beard sprouting out of her face came thundering out, Johnnie apparently chasing her.

George hurled himself on top of the pig. Johnnie thrashed about, trumpeting, but George hung on to his ears like grim death, and Johnnie stopped at last, exhausted and trembling.

"Bloody pig," George gasped, but everyone standing round was roaring with laughter. Even the Bearded Lady.

"Gracious heavens, what a fright he did give me," she said in a high-pitched, ladylike voice so much at odds with her appearance that Poll gazed at her wonderingly.

"I'm so sorry, my dear," Mother said. "It's our pet pig. He wouldn't have hurt you, though you couldn't have known that, of course. I thought he was safely shut up. I'd no idea he'd followed us to the Fair."

"Poor Johnnie," Poll said. "I expect he was lonely all by himself in the hen house and came looking for us."

She squatted down and fondled his ears. Noah Bugg said, "That your famous pet pig?" He didn't seem angry because she had kicked him but grinned at her in a friendly way when she looked up at him. Then his grin faded and Poll saw he had seen Theo, who had pushed through the laughing crowd and was standing beside her.

Theo gazed back at him steadily. Noah started grinning again. His gooseberry eyes roamed the circle of onlookers and rested on Mother.

Poll said, loudly and quickly, "I saw Johnnie from the merry-go-round. Did you see me? I was on the ostrich. It was lovely, like flying. Shall we take him home, Mother? I will, if you like, but you'd better come too. He pays more attention to you."

"No, I'll take him, unless you've had enough of the Fair already! Come along, you bad pig!" Johnnie hung his head as if he knew he'd done wrong, and the Bearded Lady gave a light, tinkling laugh and patted his head.

"He looks a bit hangdog, poor fellow," she said. "Or should it be hangpig?" Poll saw that her hands were big and strong like a man's but looked away at once; it seemed impolite to stare when she hadn't paid for it.

Mother apologized again. The Bearded Lady bowed her head graciously, said no harm had been done, lucky he hadn't knocked over a china stall, that would have been a fine how-do-you-do, and retired to her tent. The crowd began to drift away, now that the excitement was over, but Noah Bugg was still there, watching Mother intently through his pale lashes. She said, in a kindly voice, "How are you, Noah? Enjoying the Fair?"

Noah wriggled his shoulders and licked his lips nervously as if gathering courage to speak. Poll was sure he was going to say something dreadful, give Theo away, and the full horror of what this would mean suddenly struck her: if Mother knew one of her children had been telling wicked lies about Father, something would be broken that could never be mended. She pushed roughly in front of Noah and said, "Wasn't she *funny*, Mother? That voice—she sounded like Lady

March! D'you think she's a woman with a beard or a man with a lady's voice? She's fat in the chest but that could be stuffing."

"Be quiet, Poll!" Mother was frowning. She took Poll by the wrist and drew her away from the tent. "It's sad either way, the poor soul. I'm ashamed of you. She might have heard what you said. I've half a mind to make you come home with me to teach you good manners!"

"I'm sorry," Poll said. "I didn't think."

"Then you should! People like that have feelings just like the rest of us. It's bad enough that they should have to earn their livings this way, without rudeness from ignorant children."

"Yes, Mother."

"All right, then." Mother gave Poll a doubtful look as if wondering what lay behind this unusual meekness, but Poll kept her face fixed in a look of penitent sadness and Mother said, finally, "Just remember in future," and produced an extra threepence out of her purse and told her not to buy too many sweets or she would make herself ill.

When she had gone, a docile Johnnie trotting behind her, Poll giggled to herself and looked round for Theo. She wanted to tell him how clever she'd been, distracting Mother's attention from Noah, but there was no sign of him. No sign of Noah either, though Poll looked for them both for some time. She bought a toffee apple and watched herself eat it in front of a distorting mirror that made her look thin at the top, with a long neck like a swan's, and fat and spread out at the bottom, with little short legs. Then she paid a penny and went into the tooth-pulling booth to watch a boy have a tooth out. He sat in a chair on the platform with a sheet round his neck, but when the man bent over him with the pincers, he turned his back on the audience and another man played a loud tune on a trumpet so Poll couldn't hear if the boy cried or not. When he got out of the chair he looked pale and there was blood on his chin, but he smiled bravely and everyone cheered him.

George was outside the booth with a friend, looking at the notice that said PAINLESS EXTRACTIONS BY SKILLED OPERATOR. He said, "Hallo, you bloodthirsty child. Was that gruesome enough for you?"

Poll was annoyed by his superior tone. She said, "I was just looking for Theo. I thought he might be there," and George laughed again as if she had said something enormously funny.

He said to his friend, "If someone was having their legs amputated, my young brother and sister would be sure to be in the front row!"

Poll tossed her head and stalked off. George ran after her and tugged her hair gently. "Sorry, Poll, just a silly tease. If you really want Theo, he went up the church path while you were watching that painless extraction."

A young man and a girl came running down the church path toward her, gasping and laughing. The girl's strong, shining hair had come loose from its pins and hung down to her waist in thick curls, and when the young man caught her up, he picked up a handful and kissed it. She stopped laughing then and put her head on his shoulder, and they passed Poll with their arms round each other.

When they had gone it seemed extra-dark in the path, as if they had been carrying a light and had taken it with them. Poll hesitated at the churchyard gate, seeing shadows that moved as the wind tossed the trees, ghostly shapes flitting between the pale tombstones. Although she wasn't afraid—after Bride's Pit, no ghost could really alarm her—her pulses quickened a little and she was glad of the friendly sound of the Fair close behind her. As she walked between the quiet graves, she sang "Pretty Redwing" to keep her courage up.

The bright moon washed the stone of the church and whitened the grass between the moving black patterns the trees threw upon it. In the moon's light, the faces of the two boys, turned toward her, were drained of all color; their faces looked like bleached linen.

They were some way off the path, among a cramped huddle of old, leaning tombs, standing in stiff, frozen attitudes as if the approaching sound of her singing had turned them to stone. Their stillness made her nervous. She said, in a busy, cross voice, "There you are, Theo! I've been looking for you for ages!"

Theo said quietly, "Go away, Poll. Go back to the Fair."

His mouth and his eyes were dark holes in his linen-pale face. He was like some cold stranger.

She laughed awkwardly. "What are you doing here, Theo? Playing hide and seek?"

He repeated in the same dead, even tone, "Go away, Poll."

She pouted babyishly. "Not unless you say what you're doing."

"None of your business. Noah and I have something to settle."

He stared at her with those dark, stranger's eyes, and she was afraid suddenly. But how could she be frightened of Theo? She said, "You're not fighting? It's stupid to fight . . ." Her voice trailed away and the fear grew inside her.

Noah shifted lumpishly from one foot to the other. He muttered, "She's right. Let's give over."

Theo shook his head.

Noah said, "I don't want to go on. Never did." He sounded bewildered and plaintive. "It was you kep' it up, all along."

"It's got to be ended now," Theo said. "There's no other way."

His voice was stretched and taut. Like a bowstring, Poll thought—and knew he was dangerous! In this mood, Theo was dangerous . . .

She whispered, "Noah," meaning to warn him.

But he tittered, unwisely, and Theo swung round with a hissing intake of breath, fists clenched, head flung back.

Noah looked him up and down and then said impatiently, "I don't want a fight over nothing. Grow *up,* Greengrass, can't you?" and this echo of that long-ago taunt on the ice was the last straw for Theo.

He gave a sharp cry and rushed at Noah, jabbing a foot behind his calf to throw him off balance. Noah reeled, but recovered, and they wrestled together, panting and grunting and staggering in a kind of absurd, drunken dance, their arms round each other. They were evenly matched now, the same height, the same weight, but Theo was wild with rage and that gave him the advantage. He broke loose and punched Noah in the throat, a murderous blow that made Noah gurgle and gasp. Theo hit him again, in the stomach, and Noah doubled over and fell. Theo kicked him again as he lay crumpled against one of the tombstones.

Poll saw Theo's face, pale and exultant and terrible, and shouted, "Stop. Oh, stop, Theo," but although he turned his head briefly toward her, he took no notice of her anguished cry. He flung himself on top of Noah and fastened his hands round his neck.

Poll saw Noah's head rolling limply as Theo shook him up and down. Whimpering, she wound her fingers in Theo's hair and tugged hard, digging her heels into the ground and throwing her weight back. He yelped and struck at her but she hung on until she had dragged

him off Noah. Then she let go and backed away, frightened.

But Theo didn't come after her. He was standing
still, staring down. He said, "Get up, don't play the
fool," but Noah didn't move. He lay like a bundle of
old clothes on the ground. His eyes were half-closed,
rolled up under the lids, his mouth drooping open.

Poll said, "He looks dead."

"He can't be!" Theo looked at Poll and she saw
horror dawn in his eyes. He said, "Why didn't you stop
me?"

"No one could stop you."

He nodded and swallowed. The wind and the dis-
tant tune from the merry-go-round sighed in the tall
trees above them.

Poll said, "It wasn't Noah's fault, none of it. I
don't mean just now, him not wanting to fight, but
before. All that about blackmail! Noah just teased you,
that's all! You made the rest up!"

"I don't know," he said. "I don't know. It's all
muddled."

She said triumphantly, "You wanted a quarrel because he called you a runt. That's all it's been all the
time. And now you've killed him because of it."

Theo was watching her, fascinated. He said, "Poll
. . ." but she started to cry.

"Poor Noah," she sobbed. "Oh, poor Noah." Her
tears fell like rain. Poor Noah—but poor Theo, too! She
gasped out, "Run, Theo, run away quickly before some-

one finds out! Or they'll catch you and send you to prison!"

He said, very bitterly, "Now that I know what you think of me, what a mean, shabby person I am, I'd rather stay, thank you! I just hope they'll catch me and hang me!"

This made her cry harder. Through a veil of tears, Theo's face wobbled in front of her. He said, "Listen, Poll, I can't run away! Can't just leave him . . ."

She started to scream in little, short bursts. Someone shouted, "Shut your bawling, you silly great mawther!"

She stopped, choking. Noah was sitting up, grinning. She rubbed her eyes but it was true, not a dream! She said, "You were only pretending!"

"Only way to stop him, warn't it?" He got up, feeling himself very carefully as if wondering how many bones had been broken. Then he smiled slyly at Theo. "Took you in, didn't I?"

Theo frowned. Poll was afraid he was going to say that he hadn't believed Noah was dead for a minute, it was only his stupid young sister! She said, "Theo was scared to death! We both were!"

Noah beamed. Theo smiled shakily. He said, "I'm sorry, Noah. Poll was right, what she said. I made it all up! All what I told you!"

Noah thrust his hands deep in his pockets and swaggered. "Think I didn't know that? You're not the only person with brains."

"No, I know that," Theo said humbly. Now it was over, he looked very sick.

Noah said, "That's that, then. I reckon we're square now. You bashed me up and I fooled you!" He took his hand out of his pocket and offered it to Theo, who stepped forward and shook it. They looked at each other and laughed in what seemed to Poll a loud, stupid way.

She followed them back to the Fair, feeling a little resentful because they went on ahead without once looking back at her, but she was too occupied with her thoughts to be really jealous. Theo had said she would understand what he'd done when she was older, but she understood now—and better than he did! Theo was clever but he wasn't *sensible* the way ordinary people were. He saw things differently and this set him apart. Poll thought, *Theo will always be lonely,* and it made her feel proud and sad to know this, and very responsible. It was as if someone, a teacher or a clergyman or Aunt Sarah, had suddenly said to her, "Your brother will have a hard time all his life. You will have to look after him." She would have to do that, now she'd been asked, however angry she might sometimes get with him.

9

Aunt Harriet was shouting at Mother. Hesitating at the back door, Poll heard her say, "I don't care what you say, Emily, some children feel more than others and that one wasn't raised in a cowpat!"

She swept out of the kitchen, almost falling over Johnnie and Poll on the step. She was huffing and puffing with temper but when she saw Poll she laughed her loud, mannish laugh and said, "Talk of the devil! Go and put on a clean frock. We're off out, you and I!"

She whisked off, skirts flying. Poll went indoors and said, "What was all that?"

"Just your aunt having the last word as usual."

"What about? What child wasn't raised in a cowpat?"

"Never you mind." Mother was pressing a dress,

soaping the seams. The flatiron hissed as she banged it down harder than was really necessary, and her lips were compressed. She said, without looking at Poll, "Your blue and white check will do. And a fresh petticoat. She's ordered the governess cart from the Angel, so hurry up and don't keep her waiting."

Aunt Harriet was at the door, the gray pony fidgeting. It had started to rain, big, thundery drops, and with the gig umbrella up and the waterproof rug over their knees, they were warm and dry in their small house on wheels. Aunt Harriet did not seem disposed to talk but she slapped the reins on the fat pony's rump, singing "Pretty Redwing" in a strong, cheerful voice, and by the time the rain had stopped and she had folded the umbrella and put it back in its holder, she seemed in fine spirits and Poll dared to ask where they were going.

"Mystery tour," Aunt Harriet said. "Wait and see."

The governess cart rattled through lanes dusty with summer and stopped outside a cottage with a slanting roof covered with roses and a green water butt outside the back door. A plump woman came running out and helped them down from the trap. She had a chrysanthemum head of fiery red hair and her face was a round moon of freckles and laughter. She called Poll "my chicken" and clasped her to her cushiony chest, scratching Poll's nose on a brooch, then released her and cried, "Harriet, what fun, you're in time for tea!"

Outside the cottage door, in the sun, was a huge wooden box, squirming with puppies. Their mother came forward, crouching belly to earth and showing white teeth in a smile. "She won't hurt you, my chicken," the plump lady said. "You can pick up her puppies."

Poll was enchanted. Five of the puppies were smooth-coated like their mother; the sixth was covered with tight, brown curls. When Poll picked him up, he was heavy and warm in her arms, his soft stomach firm as a drum. "He'll make a fine dog, that one," his owner said. "All the others are bitches. First things first though, you'll be hungry after your journey." Poll set the puppy down and he stumbled back to the box on short, splayed-out legs, crying for his mother.

Tea was laid on a table under an apple tree. They ate bread and butter and blackberries and damp harvest cake. The two women talked and laughed and Poll watched the puppies. She liked the curly one best—he was so bold and strong, trampling his sisters to get to the side of the box and standing up to look over, and his nose shone like a black boot freshly polished for Sunday.

Aunt Harriet said, "We can't stay too long, Hetty. Better pass the time of day with the old fellow before we go, I suppose. How's he been?"

Hetty didn't answer for a minute. Poll saw her round face grow sober and somehow chilled under her flaming hair as if the sun had gone in. She said, "No better, nor will be, this side the grave," and Aunt Harriet put her hand out, over the table, and Hetty clasped it.

They got up and carried the tea things indoors. Poll offered to help but Aunt Harriet told her to play with the puppies, and she guessed that the "old fellow," whoever he was, disliked children. The door was left open and she could hear Aunt Harriet talking and a low, whining grumble replying, but all she could see when she craned her neck forward was the end of a bed with a patchwork quilt on it.

She tickled the puppies. The curly one decided her hand was a good toy to play with and attacked it in short, prancing rushes, his little teeth sharp as needles. She laughed and wiggled her fingers and he stalked them, stiff legged, growling like a small engine.

"Like to take him home, Poll?" Aunt Harriet said.

Poll's heart missed a beat. Had she misunderstood? But when she looked up, Aunt Harriet was beaming down, the bumps of her cheekbones hard and shiny as apples. She said, "Birthday present."

Poll's birthday had been two weeks earlier. Mother had given her a satchel, Theo and Lily a blue china duck full of chocolates, and George had made her a popgun, from an alder stick with the pith removed, that shot acorns or small balls of wet paper as ammunition. And the aunts had given her gauntlet gloves for the winter . . .

Had Aunt Harriet forgotten? She said, reluctantly, "You gave me those gloves."

Aunt Harriet laughed. "Do you want him or don't you?"

Poll felt giddy with happiness. But she couldn't quite trust it. Aunt Harriet was given to impulses. "Never looks before she jumps," Aunt Sarah said. It seemed rude to question her kindness but Poll knew that she must. She asked, "What about Mother?"—and dreaded the answer. Mother had always said, no more animals! They couldn't afford extra food and all the scraps went to Johnnie.

"Oh, that's all right. I arranged it," Aunt Harriet said.

Poll picked up the puppy. She was too full of happiness to speak. When Hetty said good-bye to her, she could only smile weakly and dumbly. As they set off down the lane, she felt ashamed. She managed to whisper, "I didn't say thank you."

"Your face was enough, I daresay," Aunt Harriet said, rather shortly. Poll thought she seemed sad about something.

She said, "Is your friend's husband ill?" and Aunt Harriet nodded.

"Dying, the miserable man, and punishing poor Hetty for it. Hates her because she's living and breathing and he won't be much longer. If I was her I'd tell him a thing or two but she's too softhearted. It's always the soft ones get hurt in this world and it hurts the rest of us watching them." She looked at Poll. "Thought of a name for your puppy?"

Poll shook her head.

"Hetty's a Scotswoman. Hetty MacGregor. Why not call him Mac?"

Poll tried it out. "Mac?" she said, and the curly puppy wriggled excitedly and buried his cold little nose in her neck.

Mother said, "Your responsibility, mind! Any puddles or messes, you clear them up!"

Poll said, "I'm so happy I could die. Theo always wants to die when he's miserable but I feel like that when I'm happy."

"Don't make much sense that way round," Theo said. "Can I hold him?"

"He might wet on you. He has on me, twice. And he's *hungry*. Can he have some milk, Mother?"

Mother put a saucer of milk on the hearth. Mac started to lap but stopped when Johnnie came to investigate. The huge pig terrified him; he staggered back to Poll, squeaking, and tried to climb up her legs.

"Go away, Johnnie, you've scared him," Poll said.

"Poor old Johnnie," George said. "He was here first. Come here, poor old pig, *she* doesn't want you." He sat down and scratched Johnnie's neck and blew into his ears, until he grunted with pleasure.

"I'm not pushing Johnnie out," Poll said. "It's just that Mac is only a baby and I have to look after him."

"Oh, of course!" George said. "Off with the old love and on with the new!" .

"Don't tease her, George!" Mother spoke sharply and George looked at her. They looked at each other and then, as if some unspoken thought passed between them, at Poll. George said, "Sorry, Poll," and Mother said, "So I should hope!" and went to the scullery.

George pulled Johnnie's ears, watching Poll. He opened his mouth to say something and closed it again.

Poll said, "Silly Mac, you've got to get used to our Johnnie," and put him down. This time, when Johnnie came up to him, he wasn't so frightened, just rolled over exposing his soft, beating drum of a belly. Johnnie nudged him with his flat nose and settled down in his rightful place on the hearth; the puppy sniffed at him, then, greatly daring, pounced on his comfortable stomach. Johnnie grunted and Mac started to play, dancing round him, nipping his ears, and yapping excitedly. Johnnie seemed not to mind these attentions, and when he grew bored and stood up to go, he looked back at the puppy from the door of the scullery as if to say, "Why not come along, take a look at the garden?" and little Mac cocked his head on one side and trotted after him.

"I knew they'd be friends," Poll said. "Didn't you know they would, George?"

But George didn't answer. He hadn't moved from his chair and was watching Poll with a worried, abstracted expression as if he were too absorbed in his private thoughts to pay much attention to his sister's new puppy. Was he pretending not to be interested because he was jealous? Poll knew she would have been, in his place, but George wasn't like that. "George hasn't a jealous bone in his body," was what Mother said, and Poll had always thought this a silly remark. How could bones be jealous? Perhaps George was just in a funny mood . . .

She noticed, the next day or two, that George made more fuss of Johnnie than he had done for ages. He had often complained that the pig took up too much room and was always occupying the hearth when he wanted to stretch his long legs out. Now he not only didn't complain, but came home every day with some tidbit for Johnnie: an apple or a handful of acorns. Poll began to think that even if George wasn't jealous on his own behalf, he might be jealous for Johnnie, now she had the puppy.

A week later something happened that made her quite sure of this. Breakfast was over and she was having a last game with Mac before she went off to school, throwing a cotton reel on a string for him to pounce on with fierce little growls, when George said, "What about saying good-bye to Johnnie before you go, Poll?" And when she looked up, surprised, "Well, poor old pig, you've been neglecting him lately."

She said, "Don't be stupid," but he had made her feel guilty. She loved Johnnie, of course she did, but he was old and fat now and Mac was more fun to play with. She picked up her satchel and went up the garden to make amends. But although the hen house gate was open, Johnnie didn't come trotting eagerly out as he always did.

Mother was at the back door. "Hurry up, you'll be late. Annie's come for you."

She said, "*Johnnie*," impatiently, but he still didn't come out of the hen house.

Mother frowned as she kissed Poll. "First time he's not come when he's been called in his life!"

"Just lazy," Poll said. She shouted, "Good-bye, you lazy old pig," and ran off to school.

And when she came back, he was gone.

She hadn't known—for the rest of her life she was sure she hadn't known—and yet, when she came home, she knew what had happened before anyone told her.

She was late for tea. She came in with Annie, their pockets full of acorns they had collected for Johnnie, and her family was at the table already: Lily and George and Theo and Mother with Mac on her lap. Only one missing. She said, "Where's Johnnie?"—and, in her heart, knew the answer.

Mother said, "Oh, Poll." There were tears in her eyes.

Poll's tongue was clumsy and dry in her mouth. "Where's he gone?"

Mother shook her head, apparently speechless. She put Mac down and went to the dresser to get a plate for Annie.

Lily was braver. "He went to the butcher this morning."

Poll said nothing.

Lily said, "Darling Poll, we couldn't keep him forever. A great pig, eating his head off! You knew that, didn't you?"

"I don't think she did!" George's voice shook with anger. He looked at his mother, accusing her. "You should have explained. Oh, that was *wicked*—"

"Shut up, George," Lily said.

Mother put the cup and plate on the table and sat down again. She said pitifully, "It never seemed the right time. She was so ill, and then it got harder. I was sure she must know; all her friends keep pigs, don't they? You've got a pig, haven't you, Annie?"

Poll said slowly, "Johnnie was different. You always said he was different."

"I told you, Mother!" George said.

She looked at Poll. "I'm sorry. I truly am sorry. It's been hard for us all. We all loved the old pig . . ." Her voice trailed away. Her head drooped but she lifted it with an effort, smiling sadly. "I should have talked to you, Poll. But I thought . . . well . . . I thought it might be easier for you, this way. For me too, I suppose. You know what you are! I'm sorry if I was wrong and I hope you'll forgive me. Sit down now and have tea."

Poll shook her head.

George said, "I don't suppose she's exactly hungry! I know I'm not! And I know another thing, too! I'll never eat bacon again as long as I live."

"I'm going to be sick," Theo said. He got off his chair and ran from the table.

"Nor pork, neither!" George raged. "Nor *sausages*.

179

If any *bit* of Johnnie comes into this house, I'll never eat at this table again! I'll leave home, so help me, and go to Australia!"

Lily said coldly, "There's not much chance of your eating Johnnie, George. We owe the butcher."

"Oh." George looked down at his plate. He muttered, "I didn't know."

"Well, you know now," Lily said. "How'd you think poor Mother's been managing? Have you ever *asked?* I've not noticed you holding back!"

George was silent.

"Just like a man," Lily snorted, and went round the table and put her arm round her mother. Mother took her hand and held it against her cheek.

George cleared his throat. "I could have left school. I could have got a job and brought money home."

Mother whispered, "Your education is important, dear. Sarah thinks you may get into Cambridge."

"To hell with Cambridge," George said. "To hell with Aunt Sarah!"

No one answered that shocking remark. Mother patted Lily's hand and sat straight in her chair. Lily went back to her seat and poured tea. She said, "Even if Poll isn't hungry, perhaps Annie is. Sit down, Annie."

She didn't look at Poll. None of them looked at her. Poll moistened her lips and said in a soft, amazed voice, "Annie said Johnnie was different. *Everyone* said he was different."

She sat on the log pile at the end of Aunt Sarah's garden. She stared straight ahead of her. Her eyes were hot but dry; the burning lump in her throat too solid for tears. When Annie came finally, she made room for her on the logs but took no more notice of her.

After a while, Annie said, "I don't like it when our pigs get killed, either." And added, after a pause, "But there's always plenty to eat, pig-killing time."

Poll looked at her then. Annie's face was thin, like her mother's.

She said, timidly, "Are you angry, Poll?"

"Not with you," Poll said, and knew, suddenly, that she wasn't angry with anyone. She had thought for a bit that she hated her mother but there was no point in that. People ate pigs and so pigs had to be killed. If they weren't, people went hungry.

Annie said, "I've got a bit of cake for you, Poll. Do you want it?"

"Thank you," Poll said.

She ate the cake, every crumb, because Annie had brought it, but it tasted like ashes . . .

As all food did from that moment. Like ashes or sawdust: horrible, choking stuff that dried up her throat. Even the thought of putting something in her mouth and swallowing it down to her stomach began to disgust her.

She ate no supper that evening, no breakfast the next day, no midday dinner. For tea, Mother cooked her an egg in the way she liked best, coddled in a cup with thin strips of toast to go with it, but even this favorite dish made her sick as she looked at it. Mother said, "You'll sit at that table until you do eat it, my girl," but when Poll was still there, half an hour later, she took the cold egg away without saying a word and sat down and started to make a rag doll for Mac out of an old shirt of George's.

Lily came to her room after she'd gone to bed and said, "Please, Poll, you haven't eaten for days; don't punish Mother this way, it's so cruel."

Poll said, "I'm not! I *can't* eat, not *won't.*"

"Will you drink a glass of milk, then?"

She brought the milk and Poll tried to drink it but the first sip made her gag. Lily took the glass as she doubled up, retching. "My inside's closed up," she sobbed. "Really, Lily!"

Theo said, "You'll die if you don't eat. How d'you think Father will feel, when he comes home, if you're dead and buried?"

"He's not coming."

"Of course he is. Mother's had a letter."

Poll shrugged her shoulders. Father would never come back. *Blood will out,* was what Mrs. Bugg said. And Aunt Harriet, *Some people are footloose.* Father had left them like Grandpa Greengrass had left him when he was young. She didn't blame Father any more than Aunt

Sarah had blamed Grandpa Greengrass, but the knowledge was like a sad weight in her chest. Heavier because only she knew it.

She sighed and said, "Poor Mother."

Aunt Sarah took her for a walk. She was weak because she had not eaten for seven days, and was glad to hold Aunt Sarah's hand. They went down Station Street and Aunt Sarah stopped in front of the butcher's and said, "Look, my dear, those are dead creatures hanging there and you must face up to it. They have to be killed so that human beings can live and grow strong. We are carnivorous animals. Do you know what that means?"

"Yes," Poll said. "We eat meat." And fainted dead away.

She rather enjoyed all the fuss. Someone bathed her forehead with water and when she got home she lay on the old sofa in the front room and George brought Mac to amuse her. The puppy made her laugh when he played with his rag doll, running round the room, growling, its head in his mouth, and then bringing it to her and looking up, head on one side, eyes bright as buttons, inviting her to play tug-of-war.

George said, "You should take him for a walk; the poor chap needs exercise. There's a blue leather collar and lead in the saddler's. Costs seven and sixpence."

"I haven't got any money," Poll said.

"Earn some, then!" George laughed as if a bright idea had just struck him. "Tell you what, you eat this pear and I'll give you twopence."

It was quite a small pear, yellow, with a red blush where it swelled out at the bottom.

George said, "We could draw up a scale of charges. Twopence for a pear, threepence for a glass of milk. Sixpence if you eat a whole plate of dinner. Though you'll have to work up to that gradually or you'll make yourself ill. People's stomachs shrink when they've been starved for a bit."

She ate the pear and George gave her two shiny new pennies. The next day she had another pear and a glass of milk and a sticky bun, which made sevenpence altogether. She ate her dinner and George paid her eightpence for that because she had a second helping of pudding.

By the time she had earned seven shillings and sixpence she had begun to feel ordinarily hungry again and went on eating without being paid because George said he had run out of money. The collar fitted the puppy and although he hated being on a lead to begin with, sitting down, front paws braced, when she tried to get him to walk, she coaxed him gently and quite soon he was scampering along, dragging her after him until she was quite out of breath. "Silly dog," she scolded, "why can't you be sensible and walk to heel like old Johnnie?"

Mother said, "Pigs have more brains than dogs, didn't I tell you?"

She looked at Poll shyly. She had often been shy with Poll since Johnnie was killed. As if she felt she had done something wrong and was afraid Poll would never forgive her. It made Poll feel uncomfortable and ashamed as if *she* had done something wrong. She wished she could think of something to say to comfort her mother, and not just about Johnnie, but about something much worse that she knew and that Mother didn't. Father had left them and one day, when they all grew up and went away too, Mother would be quite alone. Sometimes, when she seemed especially happy, singing while she was washing up in the scullery or laughing at some joke of George's, it made Poll's heart ache to think how lonely and sad she was going to be. She wanted to hug her and hold her close then, but she didn't. Mother would only say, "What's *that* for, all of a sudden?" and she wouldn't be able to tell her for the same reason that Mother hadn't explained what was going to happen to Johnnie. You kept the saddest things hidden from people you loved.

Poll said, "Do you remember when you put Johnnie into that pint beer mug, how funny he looked?" and her mother laughed as if she was relieved about something and touched Poll's cheek with her finger that was rough tipped with sewing.

The walnuts were ripe in the avenue at the back of the church. An old woman sat there during the week to chase the boys off, but on Sundays she stayed at home and after church they lagged behind their aunts and their mother and filled their pockets when no one was looking.

Lily said, "Dad likes walnuts. We'd better save some for him. I wonder if he'll be home in time to see me in the school play. Oh, I do hope so. Why are you pulling that face, Poll?"

"I'm not pulling a face."

"Yes, you are."

"I am *not!*"

Lily said angrily, "Do you think I'm not going to be worth seeing? Is that it?"

"No, of course not."

But it was partly that. It seemed to Poll, suddenly, that everyone was always looking forward to something wonderful that might never happen. Lily to being a famous actress, Mother to Dad coming home, Theo to being grown up, not an odd and lonely little boy but a person with friends, Father to making his fortune . . .

It was a dangerous way to go on. The only safe things to be happy about were things that were over and gone. Poll felt cold, as if she had been turned to cold stone.

"What's the matter?" George said. Then, more urgently, "What's the matter, Poll?"

They were all staring at her. She couldn't speak. Aunt Sarah had stopped and was coming back. She said, "What's wrong with you, Poll? You look as if you'd seen a ghost."

"I can't move," Poll whispered. If she took one more step, something dreadful would happen.

"Go on," Aunt Sarah said to the others. She knelt, in the dust, in her best dress, and put her arms round Poll.

Poll leaned against her. After a minute, Aunt Sarah said, "Just growing pains. That's all that's wrong with you."

Poll said, "All this . . . all this *looking forward* . . ."

She couldn't explain more than that. But it was no good telling Aunt Sarah. She was worse than anyone else, looking into the future and hoping for so much for them all. "I'm frightened," Poll said.

"Oh, you have to be brave to look forward," Aunt Sarah said. "Come on now, hold my hand." She stood up and brushed her dress down and looked at Poll keenly, as if she saw into her mind. "Things do go right sometimes," she said.

And one most important thing did. Poll went out to tea one day after school and when she came home Father was sitting by the fire, cracking walnuts.

She stood in the doorway and stared. For a second he looked like a stranger, quite an old man with gray in his hair, and the next he was just as he had been before he went away. He held out his arms and she ran and sat on his lap and hid her face in his shoulder. He said, "Oh, my baby!" but she couldn't speak. She was too embarrassed even to look at him and he held her tight and went on talking. They were all talking: she heard his voice, and Mother's, and George's, and Lily's, and Theo's, all running into and over each other like instruments in an orchestra playing a fine, happy tune. Father's fingers stroked the back of her head, feeling the bone of her skull and the hollow at the back of her neck in the way he had always done. She began to feel foolish, sitting there with her face hidden, but dared not look up in case they all laughed at her.

At last, Mother said, "Lily, come into the scullery and help me get supper. I want some potatoes peeled. George, you've got homework, haven't you? Take it into the front room and get on with it and don't waste any more time. And Theo—you run next door and tell them Father's ship docked earlier than expected and he decided to turn up without sending a telegram. Just to catch us all on the hop! Isn't that typical!"

Doors closed. Silence, except for the creep and hiss of the fire and small, squeaky sounds as Mac dreamed in his basket. Father lifted her head away from his shoulder and said, "Well, what's been happening to you?"

She tried to think. So much—but she could only remember one thing. A little pig, sitting in a pint beer mug and squealing. A bigger pig, trotting behind Mother when she went shopping. A naughty pig, stealing hot cross buns and next door's gooseberries. A famous pig, the talk of the town, sitting good as gold in the drawing room of the Manor House with his head in his hostess's lap. A portly pig, snoozing on the doorstep in the sun . . .

Johnnie, the peppermint pig, gone now like this whole long year of her life, but fixed and safe in her mind, forever and ever.

She said, "Johnnie's dead."

Father looked at her, puzzled but smiling. He cupped her chin in his hand and said, "My darling, who's Johnnie?"

About the Author

N_{INA} $B_{AWDEN's}$ unusual and intriguing books for young readers have been published to wide critical acclaim. A reviewer in *Publishers Weekly* wrote: "I'll come right out and say it. For my money, Miss Bawden can do no wrong. Her stories are a perfect blend of humor and suspense, and that's a blend difficult to achieve."

Miss Bawden herself writes: "I was born in London and lived there until I was evacuated with my school to a mining valley in Wales. During the school term I lived with various miners' families and in vacations on a farm. . . . I went from school to Somerville College, Oxford; when I left I wrote my first novel . . . for adults. . . . I started to write for children when my own children discovered a secret passage in the cellar of the house we lived in. . . ."

Miss Bawden's other books for young people are CARRIE'S WAR, SQUIB, THE RUNAWAY SUMMER, A HANDFUL OF THIEVES, THE WHITE HORSE GANG, THE WITCH'S DAUGHTER, THREE ON THE RUN, and THE HOUSE OF SECRETS.